D1475469

CURSE OF
CROWNS®

Volume Two

Blood You Will Taste

_____

By

GARRIS L. R. COLEMAN

CURSE OF CROWNS ®

Curse of Crowns Volume Two: Blood You Will Taste is a book of fiction. Names, characters, and places are the prod-uct of the author's imagination and are used fictitiously. For the events, names, and places, anything resembling real-life events, persons living or dead, and actual locations is purely coincidental.

Cover art copyright © 2020 by Garris L. R. Coleman

Cover art design and book layout by Garris L. R. Coleman

Decorative art for chapter headings by publicdomainvec-tors.org

Hardback ISBN: 978-1-7923-4181-6
Softcover ISBN: 978-7923-4182-3
Ebook ISBN: 978-1-7923-4183-0
Fill The Pages Publishing, LLC
Printed in United States of America
for more info visit
www.curseofcrowns.com
curseofcrowns@gmail.com
garrislrcoleman@curseofcrowns.com
P.O. Box 214
Gracewood, GA. 30812

~ In Memory of August Payton Coleman ~
12-25-2019

Christmas will never be the same without you,
love Mom and Dad.

Table of Contents

ACKNOWLEDGMENTS

Taking on the task of writing a novel series has been an eye-opening experience filled with even more research, tweaking, and loss of sleep this time around. Moreover, for those who are thinking about attempting to write a novel, I always say go for it. For those who are in the process, keep going and never give up. With that said, I first must start with my beautiful and awesome wife Tricia. Thank you for all the hours you spent helping me bounce ideas around, hearing me talk about this story repeatedly, and of course keeping me fed. Without your help, none of this would be possible.

A special thanks and appreciation to the editor Patsy Hinely who has a Bachelors from UGA and Masters in Education from Pennsylvania State University, she spent many hours and weekends helping me get every detail just right in the first round of edits.

A special thanks and appreciation to an additional editor Lewis Hinely Jr., Ed. D. that obtained his Education Doctorate from UGA and a B.S, M.S. in Medical Illustration from the Medical College of Georgia. And to all those who gave me feedback from the artwork to the writing, thank you for lending your precious time.

Map Of The World Vargha

Map Of The World Argon

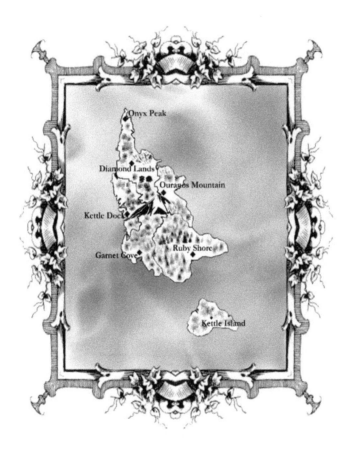

Volume Two

Blood You Will Taste

CHAPTER

1

"Closer," the shadows from the forest and all around seemed to whisper with the faint breeze. The light wind was cool against the skin. The leaves rattled in the trees as some let go and spiraled in different directions as they fell. They made a clattering sound as they hit the ground. Some scattered and scraped along the forest floor. It sounded as if hundreds of little feet were running across the dead foliage.

"Hello?" the young woman called out. She was alone, walking through the wildwood. Emerging from the tree line, she called out again and asked, "Is anyone there?"

The wind blew again as she turned to look behind. Her long stringy red hair blew across her face. The breeze blew and gave a whisper once more. She turned her head back quickly as it felt like a breath touching against her neck. Her brow tightened and eyes squinted as she took another step backwards away from the forest. The white clothing she wore was smudged with dirt stains all over, and full of wrinkles. The lower part of her dress flapped against the wind. Her skin was pale and smooth to the touch and felt as soft as cool silk.

At the edge of the forest, a large tree hung over, suspended in the air and was almost snapped in two. She walked down beside its trunk while stepping into a small crevice. The path led into a gorge of stone and granite that was vast. It had the appearance of being struck by a meteorite that had cut through the greenery and dug up even the roots of trees, destroying all that stood in its course. The young woman stopped at the path's end as she saw an opening to a cavern that the tree limbs hung over and half covered its darkened entrance. As she stood staring into it, a sparkle of purple light flickered and caught her eye, then was gone. The hissing wind blew again and made sounds to throw whispers once more. A chill came down her neck as she ran into the mouth of the cavern.

She grabbed the wall, turned and placed her back against it and slid down into a squat. She brought her knees to her chest and looked at the great openness. Tears filled her blue eyes and ran down along her cheeks. She made a sniffled as she tried to wipe them away from her face with the back of her hand. She leaned her head onto her forearms for a moment. She took deep breaths as her eyes stared off the horizon, letting her mind wander.

It was not long before the wind whistled again, but there was something different something that felt stranger this time. Again, it blew and sounded more like a warning behind her whispering, "Go…"

She stood to her feet and looked toward the oval shaped darkness as nothing was there, but another warning whispered to her and went silent as quickly as it came.

"Is someone there?" she asked, stepping along the cavern wall. Slow and careful her soft steps were as she made her way further into the darkened cave. She turned her head often to look back toward the daylight as if she did not want to leave its comfort. A flash of purple light flickered and reflected onto the stones just in front of her. The light was enticing and drew her closer. Then as she rounded one more bend, she saw the wall of light. Away from the cave's wall she stepped out to the middle of its openness and went toward its glow.

"This world has two of them," she said softly and moved closer. She reached her hand out to touch it. A gentle wave of her hand across the surface made its light ripple and swirl. Her eyes became even brighter and glowed a sparkling blue as she moved her hand in it. A half smile came across her face and an eyebrow lifted. "You didn't buzz like the other one did."

She spoke to it with gentleness as if it were a friend. One who might even consider friends of many years that had passed and not spoken for a while and now able to finally have the time to catch up with one another. The ripple from the light seemed to distract her, at least long enough to keep her tears held back. With one last swirl, she removed her hand and brought it next to her side. Strands of light began to soften and come back together as if she had not disturbed the wall of light.

She watched the ripples begin to slow, as she squinted and noticed darkened strands that looked to form a shape. *This one looks sort of like a face*, she thought and stared with deep intent. For a moment it seemed to have many faces. The darkened shape moved. A hand came through hitting her in the throat with some type of material. Her head went back as she was knocked off her feet. Into the gravel her palms scraped as she tried to catch herself.

The material wrapped around her neck and squeezed tighter as she quickly pulled at it scratching to take it off. She grasped for air and her voice strained as her face turned red. Onto her stomach, she rolled then tried to stand. The young woman thought to run away from the wall of light but fell to the ground as more of the dark material shot out and stuck to her feet and hands. The young woman struggled to breathe and fought to crawl her way to the mouth of the cavern. Her eyes looked toward the day sky, she slid across the gravel on her belly. Her eyes widened as the wind blew once more from the shadows and whispered to her, "Now you die, Your Majesty."

CHAPTER

2

"Ugh," Tessa grunted as she landed on her side. The packed and tight stitched straw roof softened her impact as she bounced. She rolled and slid down the slanted covering. Underneath were old wooden boxes stacked and used for shipping everything from clothing, weapons, and food. The locals used them for storage. The foreigners put anything they could fit in those crates for their journey back home. She tumbled on her way down and hit the roof. She turned over onto her stomach and scratched at the straw. Her hands slipped and grasped as she tried to stop herself from going over the edge feet first. A quick latching onto a rafter, Tessa's feet dangled as she gripped tighter. She leaned her head against the straw. She closed her eyes, took deep breaths, and wanted to look back up to the window to see if her Mother was still there. With a winded voice, she said, "That was too close."

Back and forth her feet kicked, Tessa tried to use her feet to feel for any kind of niche or a perch. The princess had hoped for anything to brace against to support herself. There was nothing, only plenty of air and space down below as her lower body kicked and swayed like a worm on a hook. Almost sounding like a soft prayer, she whispered over and over, "It's not that far down, it's not that far down."

Slowly she raised her forehead off the straw to look around. Her hands shook as she continued to keep a tight grip. The Princess's words became softer and softer until they were gone, and nothing more than a faint breath. Against the straw roof she opened her eyes and saw the discolored rafters. Turning her head to the side, Tessa looked at the ground anyway. "I can do this," she said. Her body eased down further. She changed her grip and lowered herself until she hung suspended. With only her fingers holding the beam, the ground was in sight. *You can let go*, she told herself for encouragement, for she was only a few body lengths from the ground now. She landed on her feet and squatted as she looked around to see if anyone noticed her.

Quickly to the wooden crates, she ran and hid

among them and peeked through the small openings. Around the corner and down the alleyway were the busy streets and markets, where everyone knew who she was. She kept her face lowered while walking through the active exchange without anyone noticing her. She knew it would be impossible for her to not be recognized. Next to her, there was a cloth bunched together. She lifted an edge with the tips of two fingers. A few bugs ran out from underneath the dry-rotted material, "That is disgusting," she said. She let go snatching her hand away.

Tessa looked around again then lifted and unfolded the old gray and torn cloth again. It looked used by a small rodent and underneath, the ground was damp and moldy. *Something could have recently used it for a home or worse, or it could still be being used.* She thought. She gave it several shakes, and brushed clumps of dirt from the inside and its filth from the outside. One final shake and a flip around the back, she covered herself. She eased to the edge of the street markets and kept her head down as she slipped amongst the crowd making her way toward a gate. She stood in line behind a family that was on their way home and waited at one of the main gates. The line that led out of the kingdom kept getting smaller. She peeked out from her hood and noticed the guards checking the hands of people. They were preventing most of them from exiting. When the guards were not looking, she stepped out of line. Tessa thought she would try another gate as she walked away.

Marching down the main road of Fog-shore, a group of eight guards headed for the main entrance while carrying long spears in their hands. She turned away and put her head down, trying to avoid them, but knocked over a stand full of food.

"What are you going to use to trade for all that you have ruined?" asked the woman that owned the stand.

"My apologies," Tessa said, as her face was still covered. She then turned to run away.

"What is this?" a guard asked as he grabbed her by the arms. She bumped into him. "I ought to take your fingers for trying to steal."

"I'm not stealing, it was an accident," she replied.

"What is your name?" he asked, snatching the cover from her head. "Princess!" he said, letting go of her and stepped back. He placed his hand across his stomach. He quickly bowed and continued, "Your father wants us to bring you to him."

"Well… I was…" she stammered, looking around. "On my way to find him…Yes, I was on my way to find him."

"Very well. We will make sure you get there. This way, Princess," he motioned, stepping to the side.

"Thank you," she replied and placed her hands at

her side and stood straight, beginning to take a step. He turned his head and fell backward into a few of the other guards. Tessa gave a quick shove, pushed him, and took off running through an alleyway.

"After her!" he commanded.

The guards gave their spears to one guard, six of them took chase after her down the alleyway. At the end of the alley, Tessa made a right, into another narrow way and ran. She made another turn, but the alleyway ended, blocked by a wall. To her left, there was a wooden door. She pushed it opened. It led into a home filled with glass windows. The natural light covered everywhere. Up the steps, she ran.

"Who is there?" an elderly voice asked, but Tessa did not stick around to answer. She had already made her way to the top of the stairs.

"Make way for the king's guard," a guard said, coming into the doorway.

The door slung open abruptly as she went up the stairs. Quickly, she ran to the railing and looked over the side. Looking to another side of the banister, she ran and climbed over its railing. She jumped to another patio and caught the top of the railing that was not a far distance. Once she was over, she tried to go through another door but found that it was locked. Through the door, a guard came out onto the patio behind her. He was a younger guard. He was getting closer and trailed not too far behind. Tessa climbed and stood on the rail, she jumped up and hung onto a beam. Her legs dangled as she strained and tried to pull herself up onto another packed straw roof. The guard reached out to grab her foot but missed as her leg lifted away from his reach. He continued after her as he climbed and stood on the rail as she did. Stopping, the guard looked and saw her standing against the wall. His head was able to peak over the roof line as he said, "It is over Princess, you have nowhere else to go. Come now, I will help you down. We will take you to your father, no harm will come to you."

Tessa turned and looked up at the top of the wall, she knew she would never be able to reach the top. Hesitant, she did not want to have that same experience her Mother went through. Her eyes looked toward the guard and then to the horizon. Her breath was heavy as she took a slow step and another toward him and said, "I do not like heights."

"It is alright, I will help you down, Princess. All you must do is simple, take my hand, that is good... a little more and you are almost there," he said, watching her, but she changed directions and ran. Out of his reach and over the edge, she made a leap through the air. For a moment, Tessa's body looked to soar as she jumped off the roof.

Into the cold sea, she plunged. Holding her breath, Tessa went feet first, and her dress came over her head while her body was submerged in the water. Sticking to her head and arms, she fought to reach the surface as she felt the weight of the dress holding her under. The current pulled her further down. She pulled a lace and wiggled her way out from the bottom. The dress floated to the top and moved with the current. Up to the surface she reached and gasped for air as she swam over to the docks.

She pulled herself in closer and wrapped an arm around and held onto one of the pier's support planks. She hung onto it with a firm grip while catching her breath. With her other hand, she felt her neck for the gift that her father had placed around her. The water rocked and shifted, lifting her up and down while splashing against her. Watching for her on the ledge above, the guard saw her dress float to the top. He turned to the others and said, "Quick! Get to the docks. I am going in after her."

Hiding under the docks, she heard the guards splashing. Tessa took a deep breath and dove under to get away from him. She used the post to push off and swam to another and only to the surface to catch a quick breath. Back under, she went hoping to lose any of them following her. The guard swam over to the dress, he pulled on it, but she was gone. He dove down and came back up. He looked around and did not see that she had come up on the other side of the dock. Hidden by the motion of the waves, she swam further away. Tessa used the docks post and hid under the pier and made her way to a different part of Fog-Shore's city.

Across her chest she placed her arm as water dripped from her body. Tessa shivered as she walked beside the docks. The waves slightly crashed against her back as she made it out of the water and near a stone wall. There, she moved throughout the village alleyways, undetected. Tessa made her way toward another exit. Down another alley, she went, the guards ran past an opening. She quickly stepped into the shadows of a doorway, avoiding them. Only half of her face was covered in the shadows as she hid, waiting for a guard's squad to pass. She looked out from the door and the light lit the rest of her face as she checked to see if the way was clear. She began to run and make a dash for another hiding spot. A hand reached around and covered her mouth, pulling her back into the shadows of the corridor.

"Ssh… Don't make a sound, okay?" the voice asked, and Tessa nodded her head. "They're not letting anyone leave, but I..." the voice whispered while uncovering Tessa's mouth.

"Oaks? Is that you?" Tessa asked, interrupting him.

"Yes," Oaks answered, softly.

"I thought you left?"

"I tried, but the guards wouldn't let me. They are blocking every entrance. I know another way out of the city. We will have to wait until evening."

"You were right, there's something not right with Father," Tessa said.

"Where is Mother?" Oaks asked.

"She is with Father. I watched him do something to her… That crown just changed. I don't understand how he could do that. Mother said she didn't want it and he just forced her. Now, I think there's something wrong with her. Why would he do that?" Tessa asked.

"Ssh… you have to talk softer," Oaks said, covering her mouth again.

"Okay," Tessa whispered, moving Oaks hand away. "Why would he do that?"

"I don't know, I watched him kill Barron. Once it becomes nightfall, we are getting away from here," Oaks said, as they both hid in the corners shadow.

CHAPTER

3

"**My apologies** Sir," Fai Yan said, offering his condolences to Taiki. With care, he handed him the bag with Seiji's head in it.

Taiki opened the bag and eased his son's head out. He dropped the cloth sack and fell to his knees while each palm held his son's cheeks. Taiki's eyebrows tightened as tears formed. He stared at his son, wishing to bring him back to life in his thoughts. Outside and around the village, the Hurons mourned their friends and family members. As tears streamed down Taiki's face, he asked, "How did this happen?"

"When we left looking for Seiji, Cai picked up a trail later in the afternoon that led us to Fog-Shore. There was no way we would have made it back before night.

Once the morning came, Elias' men were waiting outside the door. They said he wanted to see us. We went into a large room, and there Elias said he had something for you," Fai Yan replied. He paused as he wiped a stream of tears from his face. A flash of Elias holding up Seiji's head entered his mind.

"Then?" Taiki asked.

"Sorry Sir," he replied wiping his nose. "He demanded all of us to bow or we would suffer the same fate as Seiji. Cai refused and pulled out his sword along with everyone else. Everything happened so fast, that I didn't pull my sword. Elias allowed me to keep my life because of it."

Fan Yan blinked and a vision of spears plunging into his friends and his brother Genji, kept playing over his mind. The clashing of steel swords rang out in the Great Echo Hall and resounded in his mind. He wiped his tears again, and said, "Sorry, Sir... I know I keep pausing."

"It's alright Son," Taiki replied.

The room's stone floor collected small puddles of blood. Cai and his men stared up to the ceiling as their lives faded from their bodies. Some gasped for air while their mouths spit blood. The swordsmen came and finished them by cutting off their heads. Elias pushed Fan Yan down the stairs. Fan Yan looked up at Elias from the bottom step. "Next time I see you, I won't be as merciful. Now, gather their heads and take them with you," King Elias said. He tossed Fan Yan a cloth bag. Elias' words haunted him.

"I don't think I will be able to forgive myself. He made me give the order of their execution to his men."

"It was out of your control and not your fault. Don't let what Elias has done be your guilt. I'm glad you made it home safe. Son, go and be with your family," Taiki said.

"Thank you, and Sir, I'm truly sorry what happened to your son."

Taiki nodded his head giving him a peaceful sign. Fan Yan turned and went from the Pagoda. Looking down at his son, he stared and placed Seiji's head in his lap as he knelt. A pair of feet walked and stopped next to Taiki.

"Sir, you should let me take him," a young man named Lizen said. He helped keep the Pagoda clean and assisted Taiki with many things throughout the day. He brought a wooden box for Seiji to be buried in. Placing the box down, he extended his hands and reached to take Seiji's head from Taiki.

"Get out," Taiki said, with a low tone and stared with a blank face.

"Sir," Lizen said.

"I said get out. GET OUT! All of you GET OUT!" Taiki shouted.

"Sir, my apologies," Lizen said, with his head down, backing away.

"Where is he?" Misaki asked, entering The Pagoda making her way through the men that were sent out.

"We are sorry, Misaki," many of the men said on their way out.

"No… No... Not my son," Misaki said. Seeing only her son's head in Taiki's hands, she began to cry. "No, it's not supposed to be this way, where is his body?"

Misaki knelt next to Taiki. She breathed deeply and buried her face into her husband's shoulder. Squeezing his shirt, she wept as he placed a hand on the back of her neck. Wiping her eyes, she made a sniffle and reached to touch Seiji. Stroking his hair, she asked with a soft voice, "Who did this?"

"One of our groups stayed in Fog-shore last night because they wouldn't have made it back before dark. This morning, Elias had them meet with him and declared himself king of all. He told them if anyone opposes him, they will be killed. Then he held up Seiji's head. Cai and his men became enraged and Fai Yan was the only one, he..." Taiki said. He paused, staring in deep thought.

"Fai Yan was the only what?" Misaki asked.

"Sorry, Fai Yan was the only one Elias spared," Taiki said.

"I don't understand, why would Elias do something

like this? We haven't done anything to him," she said wiping tears from her eyes. "I thought we were friends. We trade with them."

"I don't understand why he would do that, and why our son was even there to begin with," he replied. His face turned a few different shades of red as the anger increased. His eyes were still filled with tears.

"I want to bring him back," she said.

"Me too. I would trade my life for his if I could."

"Elias didn't even give us a chance to say goodbye," she said.

"No, he didn't. I want to know what our son could have done to deserve this?" he asked.

"I wondered the same, but this makes me want to cut off Elias's head."

"This makes me feel the same way," he replied and looked at her. "This is going to make many of the others feel that we need to retaliate."

"For now, I want to take time and mourn for our son," she said.

"I will gather the villagers together and we will mourn the death of Seiji along with the other men who lost their lives in Fog-shore."

"Give Seiji to me and I will prepare him for burial," Misaki said.

"He is our son. I will help you prepare him," Taiki said, bringing his forehead to Misaki's forehead.

Wrapping Seiji's head in a white sheet, Taiki and Misaki placed his head into the special coffin that Lizen brought into the Pagoda. They decorated the outside of the white coffin box with flowers the color of fuchsia. Along with the other Hurons they prepared family and friends for burial.

A day passed and Taiki and Misaki along with the other families of Huron Village, took and placed their deceased into the ground of one of the hillsides. There in the fields, white Lilies grew in the summer months and pink Magnolias during winter. Gathered in the field among the Magnolia flowers, the villagers wore white silk to honor those that had fallen. As the living placed their deceased family member into the ground, everyone surrounded that person showing their support in silence. No one knew what words to speak. They all scooped a handful of dirt and covered the coffin. They lit incense and white candles to honor them. Once they were buried, the Hurons all turned and faced the sunset. With the smoke from the incense rising in the faint breeze, they watched the golden sun disappear into the horizon.

A few days had passed after laying Seiji and the other men to rest. They all continued to mourn the loss by lighting white candles in different parts of their homes.

Every villager that came and entered the Pagoda

paid their respects by bringing a single Magnolia flower and unlit white candle. They stood in groups waiting to speak with Taiki and Misaki. Many wanted to have a meeting to know what they were going to do about the fallen friends and family members. They watched Taiki and Misaki, for he was still saying prayers for Seiji and continued to mourn for him. Out of respect for them, the villagers returned to their homes.

CHAPTER

4

Mistaken for black stones that bulged from the ground, they blocked the view of many of the sandy shores. This season of the year those protruding rocks were covered with ice and filled the shoreline of the Red-Pine country as waves splashed onto its coast. Closer, the ships from Fog-shore came, and the stones revealed that their true color was a soothing dark red. The water running off the rocks and back into the sea looked like a red wine being poured from its bottle. Carried throughout the high winds, blew the strong scent of trees. They were the red pines. Sweet to the nostrils the smell was, as it filled the air all around. The locals loved the strong bitter taste that the red needles gave. They broke the needles to eat and brewed them for tea. Even the bark from the trunks were edible. Red pines grew tall, reaching great heights toward the skies. Their tops were the first to be spotted out in the deep waters from the sea.

Toward the docks, the ships cut through the open waters as local sea creatures rode the current of waves at the keel of the ship. The cold water looked ruby red flowing gently over their smooth white backs. Their dorsal fins and blow holes broke the surface as they swam, keeping ahead. The frigid wind blew, and the great sails ruffled and filled as the lines tightened, and they were pushed onward. A total of six massive ships made up the trading fleet. To the docks connecting to the oceanside they went carrying items for exchange. Above the mast flew a long banner of black with two swords crossing that were white and represented the act of trade.

Red Pine's docks were similar to those of Fog-shore. They were almost built identically except their arrangements of living did not have a wall surrounding them, nor did they need one for strange creatures, monsters, or the Cursed had never ventured over any of the oceans into their lands. Eerie tales of being out to sea, and bizarre myths from the distant lands were the only lore that had made it that far east. For some, they wondered and questioned if the allegory was true and to be believed? After all, neither were stories of the big ships from Fog-shore ever true...

but there they sat, floating and anchored next to the docks. The ships had sailed across the seas, filled with locals, and ready for trade. Along the shoreline and into the terrain of the pines, their kingdom of homes was built and scattered throughout the woods. Many were dug into the ground while others made theirs above lands towering with the trees.

It was late afternoon when the ships had arrived. The locals had fires burning and those on the dock rushed to help secure the ships against the boarding docks. The skies were clear and bright. Even the shorelines were calm.

"Welcome back Sir," the male's voice greeted them as it came forth from thick furs around a smooth face.

"I imagine everything is in order and staying on track?" Mason asked, as he had stepped off the wooden plank and onto the docks. His breath was sharp as it escaped into the air.

"Of course, as always, Lord Mason," the man replied, he stepped back to make room for Mason to walk. "Your plan is fool-proof."

"Very well, very well… Let us hope it remains that way." Mason reached over, patting him on the neck and side of his face. He reached into his pocket and pulled out some coin. "Now fetch me something warm to drink. I may be fat like the seals, but my bones are knocking from cold."

"Aye, Sir," he replied.

"And bring it fast, now hurry along," Mason said, he rubbed his thick hands together then shoved them inside his clothing to keep warm. The brown edges of his wool coat crossed and bunched together as he wrapped them in front of his large stomach. He walked to the edge of the docks with many of his crew members and stood. He watched as they stepped onto the dry lands to buy and trade. They all dispersed as new members boarded ready to work. Some had made the Red Pines their new home and only traveled back and forth. The crew worked long shifts as they stood guard and faced the cold days and nights laboring on the ship. As the others took their leave, the crew members who were left behind made the ships ready to leave and kept them ready to cast off at a moment's notice. Most of the work was trading with locals and not letting the ice accumulate on the rails, decks, and around the rudder.

Down the slope and toward the docks with both hands clenched around a chalice, the young man came running toward Mason. Almost breathless and panting, he reached out his hands while saying, "Here you are Sir, your hot pine-brew just the way you prefer it."

"Ah! There we are… just the thing I needed to warm my insides," Mason replied, taking a slow sip.

"You did very well, Teek."

"You weren't lying when you told me you like to cut things close. I honestly didn't think you were going to make it back so soon."

"I know how long it takes my men to make that long journey," Mason said.

"Well, Master Calder doesn't like to be kept waiting very long," Teek said as he turned and pointed up the hill. "Come, I will take you to him."

"After you," Mason replied and followed the young man.

Several men wearing armor the color of nickel followed behind them. Up the hill they went and through the pines. The young man named Teek led them on the narrow path. Wood slates placed in the ground for footsteps spiraled down the slope and into a deeper valley. The narrow path took them up another ascent until it reached a home that was made of grass and wood. It did not look very pleasant as it led into the ground. Once through the ragged opening of grasses hanging and covering the entrance, the home opened to a large size and revealed that it was carved deep into the side of the rocky height.

Torches burning with an orange flame along the walls lit the entire home. Stairs led down from the entrance balcony on each side and into a spacious room. The ceiling and walls were that of the dark red rock, held together by the roots of Red Pine trees. Toward the balcony's edge Mason walked and looked over the carved railing. A young woman with straight blonde hair wearing dark clothes approached with her hands down at her side and asked, "Master Calder would like you to follow me to the feasting table?"

Mason looked over at Teek. The young man responded with a slight nod motioning his hand toward the lady. Down the stairway and through a frame with Red Pine roots still alive on either side, they passed by rooms with closed doors. The orange light flickered on their faces and lit the way as they each walked by and into the last room. The young woman came to a chair and slid it out from the table and said, "My master will be out of his room soon, please have a seat and enjoy his wine and food."

The young woman stepped back from the chair as Mason came to the chair. There were men gathered around the table already. Their hands were breaking apart some of the meat from bones and drinking. He eased into his seat and watched; he did not even bother lifting a mug. His armed men stood with their backs against the walls at attention. Mason turned to ask the young woman a question, but she had already made it to the hallway. She pushed open a door and went through.

Around the corner at the end of the hall the young

woman stopped and knocked on the door. It was half opened, and indistinct voices were chatting. The young woman interrupted them as she spoke saying, "Excuse me Master Calder, but everyone has arrived."

"Very well, please have my daughter join us," Master Calder's voice replied.

"Yes, Master," the young woman replied and left.

Master Calder sat on a cushioned chair made from the Red Pines. He stared at his reflection in an old poorly made mirror. His shoulder length hair was white and thin as a soft cotton. He turned his head and looked at the middle of the mirror and leaned forward to wipe off a smudge, but it was across his face and next to his pointed nose. His beard matched his hair. He lifted his head, scratched underneath his chin, and adjusted the material around his small neck. His wife stood behind him trying to fasten his collar.

"Hold still," she said, losing one end. "You're squirming too much. I won't get it hooked."

"I don't see why I have to meet with him, I don't even like him," Master Calder replied.

"I'm going to end up sticking you, if you don't remain still," she replied and grabbed the other end of the burgundy material. She enjoyed helping her husband to dress and look nice. "All you have to do is hear what he has to say."

"And watch him eat my food and drink my wine,"

he said and grunted, turning his lip.

"You don't have to do what he wants," she said, hooking the material together. "There you go, all fastened."

"Good! Then I can take this ridiculous looking thing off and tell them to go back home," he replied.

"It's the latest fashion and everyone has named them neck-flaps," she replied and ruffled it. "And those people out there are your guests."

"Well, I hate it. They serve no purpose. What's a neck-flaps? Looks more like a choking hazard if you ask me. Although, I hate the guests even more. Maybe, they all can wear one and I can choke them?"

"No, we are not choking anyone. Come. Let's not keep our guests waiting any longer," she replied and tied a black ribbon around her long hair. It was straight with a mixture of gray and some black.

Master Calder stood to his feet and followed his wife toward the door. She was much shorter than he was, but behind the scene it was, Mistress Ella who held everything in their family together. He preferred having her make most of the decisions. Her happiness was what made him most happy. Even with her hair pulled up it reached the middle of her back and caught his attention as he watched her from behind. She walked with a straightened back and hands folded together in the front. Quietly waiting and meeting them at the end of the hall, was their only daughter. She was just a little taller than her mother and had her father's quick wit. She smiled as her parents stopped next to her.

"Are you ready, Beautiful?" her father asked. That was what he had always called her from the time she was born.

"I'm nervous," she replied, and held out her shaking hand.

"Let me take a look at you, Alondra," her mother said, as she grabbed her hands and raised her daughter's arms out to the side.

Alondra smiled again as her eyes lit up. She turned and lifted the bottom of her dress off the floor and spun to show off its ebony lace and mahogany ruffles. Her stringy black hair twirled and fell back to her shoulders when she stopped. She placed her hands at her side and asked, "Do you think he will like me?"

"He would be a fool not to," her mother replied placing her hands on her arms. "Remember, to keep your back straight."

"Shall we go and meet him?" Master Calder asked and extended his arm to his daughter.

"Yes," she replied and took hold of his arm with a grin.

"Now, don't smile too much," he said.

"Yes, Father," she replied.

The doors opened and a servant announced their name as they entered. Everyone stood as they walked toward the table in the feasting room. Master Calder escorted his daughter to the chair that was waiting for her. There was an empty chair next to it.

"I don't see him, Father. Which one is he?" she whispered to him.

"Maybe they are going to announce him," he replied softly.

The chair slid in as she looked up at her father and sat down. A grin came over her face as her eyebrows raised, it was not like the other happy expressions as before and her father knew that the smile was an artificial one. The thought of seeing her disappointed made him more agitated, but he kept his harsh comments restrained. He went to the end of the feasting table and sat.

"You're not eating? Is there something wrong with the food?"

"No, I'm sure the food is good," Mason replied as he sat with his arms crossed.

"So, you don't want to eat?" Master Calder asked.

"No, I'm here on more pressing matters," he replied. Alondra's interest peaked as she looked over at him. "I'm here about the coin…"

"Why don't you tell my wife another one of your stories about the wild creatures that come from your lands, she loves hearing about them," Master Calder said interrupting him. His daughter looked down to her plate and twirled her fork moving her food around.

"It has come to my attention that you are not interested in the coin, and think it won't benefit you and your family, Sir?" Mason asked.

"I have everything I could possible ask for. Why should I disturb such a good thing on something that may not work?" he asked.

"The coin is going to happen, and…" Mason replied, but was interrupted.

Mistress Ella was seated across the table from him and asked, "So, help me understand this correctly. You are not here for the betrothal of our daughter to Elias's eldest son Isidore?"

"No, I'm not here for that, they know nothing of any kind of arrangement," Mason replied.

"Then why are you here? My husband has already told you once before we are not interested in your coin scheming."

"Your husband said he was not interested in letting me trade coin for your daughter. I'm only here about the coin and to convince you to change your mind," Mason replied.

"My daughter is not for purchase!" Master Calder said as he slammed his hand onto the table.

"And I disagree. Everything you see has a price," Mason replied.

"We were told this meeting was for my daughter's betrothal, and we see no sign of Isidore and since this meeting is not, I think you need to leave! And do it now! Before I have my men throw you out."

"You were told this was about a betrothal because that's what I paid your people to tell you with the coin you have no interest in," Mason replied and lifted a hand. His men drew their swords and began attacking Master Calder's men that were along the wall. Some of them placed swords against the men's necks that were sitting at the end of the table. "I told you everything has a price and you are standing in the way of profits to be gained, lands to be obtained, and people to be enslaved."

"They will never go along with this," Master Calder said.

"I will take it by force if I have too, but some have already agreed, isn't that right?" Mason asked.

Master Calder had a confused look as he did not know how to respond. The sound of footsteps scraped against the floor as he turned his head and saw the young servant holding a small dagger in his hand. He went and stood behind the Mistress Ella and placed the dagger against her throat.

"Get away from her," Master Calder said.

"There we go again with all the demands. Can't you see you are no longer in charge?" the servant replied.

"Why are you doing this Teek?" Master Calder asked.

"I wanted you to know that it was me who arranged all of this… this meeting, your daughter's make-believe betrothal, and even down to this delicious meal. It was me. Me, me, me. All of it. With the riches I have received, never again will I be anyone's servant," Teek replied.

"Which one of these men do we spare?" Mason asked.

"The ones who are holding their mugs on the table," he replied, Mason's men thrust their blades forward running their swords into the necks of those who were not holding their mugs.

"And what do you want to do about Master Calder?" Mason asked as his men surrounded him with swords drawn.

"I would like to see him as a slave, but if we let him live others may try to come to his rescue. But first, I want him to watch his wife die," Teek replied and pulled her head back exposing her throat She made a quick gasp and did not blink as she looked toward her husband.

"Please don't," Master Calder said, but it was too late. The servant Teek slit her throat. Her head fell forward onto the plate, blood ran onto the table and down her chest.

"I told you, everyone and everything has their price," Mason said, standing to his feet.

"I want to see his life fade from his eyes as you kill him," Teek said.

"If that's what you want," Mason replied and motioned his hand.

Mason's men took turns stabbing Master Calder as Teek stood looking into his eyes. In the chair, his body went limp. Teek placed his hand on Master Calder's face and turned it as blood came from his mouth and he was motionless. He looked over at the daughter and back to Mason, started to go toward the door and said, "She is all yours."

"You all know what happens next in this land, now make sure it doesn't fail," Mason said. The men pulled their swords and headed for the doors to leave.

Alondra had buried her face into the clothing of her mother's back and cried. She wrapped her arms tightly around her waist and clenched the soft velvet in her fist and held onto her mother. With closed eyes, she could not bring herself to watch the men stab her father. She hung on tighter and shut her eyes as she heard each blade pierce her father's flesh. The old wooden chairs scraped against the floor as all the men stood and most of them left. Alondra opened her eyes quickly after feeling a finger brush her hair back off her face. She swung her hand and sat up and screamed out saying, "Don't touch me!"

Mason grabbed a handful of her hair as she tried to swat at him again and pushed her head down to the table and leaned his weight against her. His face came close to hers as she was pinned down and found it difficult to breathe. His muggy breath was warm and stunk from the warm drink earlier. Her small body trembled as he spoke saying, "You belong to me now!"

"You're hurting me," she replied and tried to breathe. Her ribs were pressed against the tables edge. "I can't breathe."

Mason let her up and slung her to the ground and stood over her. He stepped on her dress and trapped her. She could hardly move her legs as she wanted to get away but was unable. He removed his coat and said, "No one is coming for you and your father should've taken the coin."

"But, I'm to be Isidore's wife," she replied looking up at him.

"Not anymore, he knows nothing of you. To be perfectly honest with you, he is not even old enough to marry yet. But don't worry, we are already preparing a bride for him when the time is right. And it will be with a little surprise," he replied.

"What? To kill him like you did my parents," she said.

"You could say that," he replied.

"You didn't have to kill them," she said.

"Oh, but I did and now my men are already in place and will be taking over this land before the day is over. One thing you will learn is, in this life or the next, never trust a Bargolian," he replied and reached down to picked her up. "Like I said, you belong to me now."

"Don't touch me, you fat pig!" She screamed and kicked her feet, but he was too powerful for her. The threads of her dress made a ripping sound as she screamed.

Alondra's voice carried throughout the room and into the hallway as the doors opened and the guards took her out of the room. She screamed and tried to fight but there was no way they were going to let her out of the irons. Mason snapped back from his vision of her from many years ago and watched her being led away. The councilmen could not take their eyes away from her. She screamed louder and kept repeating the same two lines, "I want my sack of coins, and I hate you, . . . you fat pig!"

CHAPTER

5

The union was an occasion for celebration that lingered on throughout the rest of the evening and into midnight hours. The Tavorians continued toasting the young couple, resulting in more drinking and feasting that lasted for several hours, even after the couple left to consummate their marriage. Sailing off to Kettle Island where only newlyweds were allowed, Ollie and Cora stayed in a romantic suite just off the seashore with a view of every day ending with the dark, orange sun setting over the ocean. The waves crashed onto the white sandy beach creating a relaxing tone. Trees rattled in the constant breeze.

While they were away, their families, along with friends, came together and built them a new home so that when Ollie and Cora returned, their marriage would not have any strain and they could begin a prosperous, new life. This way of life kept Tavorians united, peaceful, and in harmony with each other. All Tavorians lived in abundance and none went without. Returning to their home from Kettle Island three months later, Ollie and Cora were greeted by their families and friends. With congratulations and gifts given to them, their new home was presented to say a warm "Welcome back."

After this welcoming, they were both excited to be back and to start their new lives together, although they did miss the view and being at Kettle Island.

While they were putting away their gifts, evening came, and Ollie walked over and began pulling Cora's hair back from her neck. His kisses gave her chills as she giggled and turned toward him. She placed her arms around his neck and kissed him back. He picked up Cora while their lips touched, he carried her off to their room. Following their wonderful night with each other, Ollie and Cora awakened in their new home: together, for the first time.

"Good morning Beautiful," Ollie whispered when Cora turned over, avoiding the soft morning light on her face as the shine filled the room.

"It's morning, already?" Cora asked, with her eyes barely open.

"Yes."

"Good morning, were you watching me sleep again?" Cora asked, giving Ollie a kiss as she snuggled next to him.

"Yes… I love watching you sleep," he answered, moving her hair behind her ear.

"How long have you been awake?"

"Long enough to watch your nose make a funny twitch while you slept."

"My nose does not twitch while I'm asleep," she said.

"Yes, it does."

"No, it doesn't," she argued.

"How do you know you don't? You're asleep."

"You're making that up," Cora said, pulling the blanket up over her nose to hide her embarrassment.

"I think it's cute," Ollie said, pulling the blanket down to uncover her face.

"Well… you can't watch me sleep, anymore," Cora said, pulling back on the blanket to cover her nose.

"You can't stop me from watching you sleep," he said, tickling her for a moment.

Cora's eyes became enlarged and her voice amplified, "I can-Ha!" Letting out a scream as she squirmed and laughed, trying to keep Ollie from tickling her.

"I can-ha!" Ollie said, playfully, mocking her.

"Just get up," she said, trying to nudge him out of bed.

"Come on... can we just lay here all day?" he asked, rubbing the soft skin of her jawline.

"No," Cora said, grabbing his hands. "We can't lay around all day..." she teased, sitting up with a bedsheet wrapped around her. "Besides, don't you remember, we are meeting Bralgon today." Cora said as she began to get out of bed.

"We have time before we have to leave," Ollie said, grabbing Cora's waist pulling her back into the bed tickling and kissing on her neck.

"We can't be in bed all day..." Cora said, with a laugh, giving Ollie a kiss and trying to pull the blanket over their heads.

"SO... how are the newlyweds?" Bralgon asked.

"Ah!" Cora screamed, jumping out of bed quickly, taking the bed sheets along with her.

"How long have you been standing there?" Ollie asked, scrambling to cover himself.

"Not long, only enough to hear a little of your romance. Not bad... not bad," Bralgon said, congratulating Ollie.

"What are you doing?" Ollie asked.

"You left your door open. Here, get dressed, Dahlia's not going to dig itself. Let's go," Bralgon said, throwing Ollie some clothes. "Oh, good morning, Love," he said, giving Cora a wink and closing the door behind him.

"Did that just really happen?" Cora asked standing, wrapped in a bedsheet, embarrassed and shocked, turning toward Ollie.

"Yes… I'm afraid so."

"Why would he do that?"

"That's Bralgon," Ollie said, nodding his head.

"We're definitely going to have to lock the door from now on," Cora said.

"Well, at least your goods weren't hanging out," Ollie said, pulling up his pants.

"Here's your shirt," Cora said, handing it to him and looked around for her clothes.

"We will be out here waiting for you," Ollie said, leaving the bedroom.

"Okay, I'll be out shortly," she replied

CHAPTER

6

"Lord, Elias will not be back for a little while, I assume. I shall return when I'm needed again," Ty said, everyone in the room had remained silent after the door had shut and guards took the woman in chains from Red-Pine away.

"Remember to not keep Lord Elias and the rest of the council waiting," the oldest member of the council replied. His name was Gus, but everyone one called him Old Man Fish. He was slim and walked with a limp and slightly hunched over. His hair was white and almost gone on top. It looked soft as the clouds while the hair on his thin jawline hardly covered his face in his old age. When he was not with the council and having meetings, he spent most of his time casting a line to catch fish. Angled toward the other men, he sat at the end of the table and closer to the door with a brown thin hide covering him for warmth.

"Don't worry Old Man Fish, I will be back and won't keep you waiting. I'm sure you got some fish to catch and fry," Ty replied and rested his hand on the old man's shoulder. He looked over at Mason with a tightened brow and then pointed to the dead man on the floor and said, "Since this is your mess, I don't care who it is, you or your men… clean it up before Lord Elias sees it."

Mason did not speak a word but only exhaled a quick breath to himself and watched as Ty went out and closed the door behind himself. A few moments went by and Mason followed him out and went to find some of his men. Down the narrow walkways and around several corners of the city of Fog-shore, Ty made his way and stopped at a dark brown door. He gave it a few knocks and waited. The latch rattled as it slid against its brackets and unlocked. A woman with her face half lit from the sun, peeked through the cracked door.

"Open up, Carmela, it's me," Ty said.

"I'm surprised to see you so soon," Carmela said. She was his wife.

"I won't be long," Ty replied. "How is he?"

"He's refusing to eat anything," she answered.

"I will speak with him," he replied.

"What are you doing here? I thought you were going to be with the council for most of the day."

"It seems Elias's sons have gotten themselves into some type of trouble. I just decided to come back for a little while until I'm needed," Ty said, he took off his coat and walked toward the back room.

"He's in the bed resting," she said, and eased opened the door.

The room was lit from day light as the door was being held open. Ty came and stood next to the bed and looked down. He placed the back of his hand onto the man's forehead and said, "Father, you're warm and you need to at least take something to drink. It will help cool you down."

"Mmm," his father only grumbled and did not open his eyes.

"And keep the cool rags on you," Ty said and placed the cloth back onto his forehead and one around his neck. He lifted his father's head and brought a cup to his dried lips. "Here, try to sip, I promise it will make you feel better."

The soothing liquid ran down and over the edges of his mouth as he did not drink any of it. Ty eased his father's head back and dried his chin and neck. He stood and placed a hand onto his father's chest then went out of the room. His wife followed him out and closed the door behind and said, "He's been like this all morning."

"It won't be long now, before he is no longer with us," Ty replied, and looked at a shelf. It had trinkets on it that his father had kept over the years. They belonged to Ty's mother. "He has come down with the same thing my mother died from."

"I will stay with him until he passes," she replied, her hands slid around his waist from behind as she leaned her head against his back. "When do you have to return to your meetings? You could sit with him for a while."

"Soon, I suppose," he replied.

Carmela let go of him and went over to the table and sat. Ty looked around the room at his father's things and remembered many of the trinkets from when he was a just a boy. He reached out a hand and moved a few of them around, picking them up. Memories of both his parents together came flooding in as one of the trinkets sparkled in the daylight. He stood still looking into its reflective shine. A blue hue filtered through the windowpanes.

"Are you alright?" she asked, as he stood in deep thought.

"I thought for a moment my father would get better, but after seeing him today, I know he is not coming back from this," he replied and came closer to the table.

"I will stay with him until the end, that way you can continue your meeting with the council."

"I'm really starting to hate that man," Ty said.

"He's your father and took care of you, why would you say something like that?" she asked.

"I'm not talking about him, I'm just thinking out loud," Ty replied.

"Well, who are you referring to then?"

Ty placed the crystal trinket back on its shelf and went over to the table. She leaned and moved his thick coat from the chair for him to have room to sit. He pulled the wooden chair out further and sat at the table with her. He rubbed his forehead massaging the skin and said, "I was referring to the council man Mason."

"Don't you think hate is a little strong to say?" she asked.

"All he talks about is the coin. He brought two people in to prove that they would do anything for coin. One of them tried to stab Mason but missed and ended up killing the other one," he replied.

"What did Elias say about it?"

"He didn't see it because he had to leave, and we all went into the council chambers."

"Are you going to tell Elias what happened?" she asked and grabbed his hand.

"I don't think he is going to be pleased when he finds out how Mason has been conducting himself and what he's trying to accomplish," he replied.

"What do you think…" she began to ask when a knock on the door interrupted her.

"Are you expecting anyone?" he asked.

"No," she replied. "Are you?"

"Not that I'm aware of," he answered and stood. He went over to the door and opened it.

On the other side of the opening out in the alleyway, a guard in silver amour stood holding his helm under his arm. The guard had shoulder length hair that was a light brown. He bowed his head with respect and said, "Forgive me Sir, Lord Elias has returned and is requesting the council right away. He says it is urgent."

"We shall leave at once," Ty replied, and looked at his wife. "I must go now. I will see you later this evening."

"I will be here," she replied.

The guard stepped back as Ty came out the door. He walked with haste as the guard followed behind. Around the corner in a hurry toward the council chambers, Ty went back the same way as earlier. The guard behind him put his helm back on and put his hand on the hilt of his sword. He kept it from knocking against his newly fitted gray armor that had a dulled nickel look. Out of his sheath, a sword slid slowly against its metal scabbard. It made a tinging sound and rung out as the tip tapped the scabbard's locket. A quick look over his shoulder, Ty saw the guard with his head down and turned back to go around another corner. A silver blade covered with a dripping red protruded from his back. Against the wall another guard quickly shoved a forearm across his chest pinning him to the wall. He jabbed a shorter blade rapidly and several times into his stomach. The guard that was behind Ty came up and pierced him through his clothes and into the side. With a tightened grip, he twisted the hilt and held the blade in place keeping Ty from moving. The young council man bled from his mouth and gasped for air as his diaphragm was prevented from moving.

Footsteps scraping against the stone alleyway as Ty's eyes looked over and followed the big man wearing a thick hide. The fur was long with thick hair and had the appearance of a small beast. The fur had no face but bore long fangs. He approached closer as the fur's skin continued to cover his head and face. He had a dagger in his grip with dark red rubies placed in its golden handle. In the other one, he flipped a coin and caught it.

Ty coughed as the man stopped and stood in front

of him. The hand with the dagger flipped in his hand and the blade went in between the fur's teeth and lifted revealing the man's face under the skin. It was councilman Mason with a sour face. He cleared his throat and flipped the coin one more time and spoke saying, "I want you to know a few things about what just happened before you die. First, I know how to keep you alive with these blades. It was a technique I learned while I was torturing those in Red Pine, so I could learn about everything. Once they are removed you will bleed out, but don't worry, I won't let that happen yet. Secondly, surprise... I did warn you, boy. I will not be taking orders from anyone here. I told you that you would be surprised what others will do for coin. Now you know what Elias's men would do for coin. Something else I want you to know... I know of your father's sickness."

Ty's eyebrow tightened as he took in a struggling breath. His teeth showed as he tried to bear the pain, then coughed. His voice strained as he remained still and asked, "How... do... you... know that?"

"Because it was I who poisoned him and before that, I poisoned your mother," Mason replied, and smiled. "The last thing you will learn in this life or the next is 'never trust a Bargolian'."

"He has a wife," the guard said.

"Okay, okay. I lied. Make this the last thing you will

learn. I will take care of her," he replied and placed the dagger up to Ty's neck.

Ty grunted as Mason slid the blade across his skin. It opened easily, like a fillet fish. His head went forward and spilled blood down his chest and on to the stone below. The guard twisted the blade as he pulled it out of his side. Ty fell to the ground and over to his side as his body went limp. Mason stepped back and said, "Make sure he stays dead."

"Yes Sir," the guard replied, and stuck Ty a few more times. "He's dead, Sir. No one can come back from those wounds, much less remain still and let others stab at them."

"Good, now to find his wife," Mason replied.

"She's in the home that he just came from," the guard replied.

"Is she alone?" he asked.

"I do believe so, Sir. There wasn't anyone around when I was at the door and convinced him to come here," the guard replied.

"Let's go and wait outside the door," he replied.

A moment later, a few knocks came on the door. It had not been long since Ty had left her in his father's home. The latch slid across the metal and his wife opened the door without looking and said, "You left your coat."

The door flung opened as the dark figure covered

in the fur pushed it open further and barged in. The wood slammed against the wall and the door almost closed by itself again. Ty's wife wanted to run away but shouted instead as he grabbed her. Mason covered her mouth to silence the scream. One of the guards reached over, pulled the door closed, and held it shut.

CHAPTER

7

"**W**ait here, I will be right back," Oaks said. He eased to the entree way.

"Where are you going?" Tessa asked. She grabbed him by the arm to stop him. "The guards might see you."

"I'm going to get you some clothes to change into. Your clothes are still wet, and you can't wear what you have on when we leave."

"Be careful," she said.

"I will," he replied. "Stay hidden in the corner, its darker there. It will take a few moments so don't leave from here. I will try not to take long. Here… take my sword."

"What am I supposed to do with that?" she asked.

"Hopefully nothing. It's one less thing that I must

carry in case I need to run. It will be easier for me to sneak around the market without being noticed. But, if you need to use it, slice with the sharp side," he replied.

"Will you bring something nice for me to wear?" Tessa asked. Her arm was across her chest as she shivered. "Maybe something that covers my arms. I'm getting colder."

"It won't be like one of your dresses," he replied.

"Can you at least make sure the clothes don't have a rodent living in it?" she asked, unsheathing the sword. She went over to the dark corner and squatted down.

"I will make sure you are at least able to run in it," he replied and stopped at the threshold.

Oaks peeked around the corner and darted down the alleyway along the wall. Others from their kingdom were carrying out trading as usual. The sound of wind blowing made a high pitch whistle as it did often near the kingdom's embankment. A constant crashing against the stonewalls, the sound of waves splashing filled the background as water fell and gushed back to the sea. Tied to the docks, the wooden ships creaked while rocking in place. Other villagers walked across the wooden planks, loading and unloading crates as they worked. Squawking seagulls flew above circling the bunched sails while searching for their next meal. Standing next to a table, a man chopped fresh fish on a block and threw the scraps to the birds.

When no one was looking, Oaks carefully eased under and crawled to another table. Feet scuffled all around him as he made his way. The cloths hanging over the tables did not reach to the ground but covered most of the way downward. At the end, he peeked between the tablecloths. His eyes scoured the area and looked to see if any guards were around. He watched those who passed by and kept checking to see if anyone else might would have seen him move from underneath the table.

He pushed the cloth aside and eased out from below with his head lowered and eyes cutting to the side. Through the crowd and bumping shoulders with the locals, he moved away from them and stood near a rack next to a stack of folded clothes. There, he tried to blend in with the fabric as he hid part of his face. He pretended to be interested in things from the market and looked away and down to avoid eye contact with anyone. None of the villagers seemed to pay him any attention as many crowds walked by continuing out their daily lives.

Near a rod with hanging clothes, he stared and waited to take hold of a stack of dark material that was on a shelf against the wall. Oaks almost picked up the material when a stern male voice spoke out.

"You, Sir," the voice said. Oaks pulled his hand

back and stepped behind toward the back with ease. He dropped to a squat behind the cloth rack. It was a guard with his hand on the hilt of his sword. Oaks peeked through a small opening between the fabric. Behind the guard who spoke stood three more guards with him. Oaks recognized two of them, they were from the unit that rode out to the cavern.

"Yes," the local man answered. He made his living by trading clothes. He was an older gentleman that threaded leather straps to armor. His daughters made necklaces made with seashells and clothing for the different seasons. "What can I do for you?"

"King Elias would like to speak with you," the guard replied. "I'm going to need you to come with us."

"I have no one to trade my things if I'm gone. My wife and daughters are collecting shells and will return soon. Can we wait until they return?" he asked.

"If your life is gone, you won't be able to trade either. Best not keep the King waiting," the guard replied and unsheathed his sword halfway showing the blade. He stared at the old man gripping the hilt tighter.

"Let's not keep him waiting," he said and took a step out from around the table.

"You, stay here," the guard said commanding another guard. "Make sure his things remain here until his family returns."

"Yes, Commander," the guard replied.

None of the guards had spotted Oaks as he was still squatting behind the rack of clothes. His back was against the wall and he could not move without being seen. The Commander guard led the older man with guards on each side of him. One guard stepped behind the tables and stood watching forward and waiting for the old man's family to return.

This could take a while, Oaks thought. as he remained crouched and silent. A peek through the linen, he looked for the other guards, but they were gone with no others in sight. He eased to his feet and reached around the rack to grab some clothes. The guard still stood looking forward as Oaks brought the stack around and crouched again. He opened them up to see if they were something that Tessa could wear. Into a ball, he bunched them together and grabbed a few more things as he eased them from the rack. Each time he watched as the guard did not move.

Oaks stepped toward the table and got as close as he could to its cloth. With one hand he threw a crumpled piece of fabric to make the guard turn his head. The garment hit the stand with the hanging necklaces made from shells. The rack made a rattling and clinging sound as it rocked back and forth. Under the table and behind the cloth, Oaks darted and hid while the guard turned. The guard was big and slow as he knelt, the guard picked up the cloth and curiously examined it. A moment passed and the guard went back to position. A female spoke and asked, "What are you doing?"

"I'm watching all these things until the old man returns or his family," he replied.

"Well, I'm his wife. Where did he go?" she asked. Her gray hair was hanging out from the white head band, blowing in the wind. Her daughters and granddaughters were walking up behind her. Some had buckets of shells and others had a net tied around a pole carrying fish they had caught. "And what are you doing with my cloth?"

"King Elias has requested to see your husband. As for the cloth, it fell over. I was only picking it up," he replied. He extended his arm to hand her the cloth.

"What does he want this time? More straps for his guards' armor?"

"You will find out soon enough when your husband returns," he replied and stepped out from among the table.

Oaks eased to the end of the tables getting ready to dart to the next set of tables. He used the sound of them talking to hide any of his movements. More of the lady's family came and stood near the table. Surrounded, Oaks leaned over and peeked under the cloth. Only the tops and sides of their shoes could be seen as they stood. Some did not wear shoes and had sand on their feet from being on the sandy shores. A thud sounded as the buckets of shells hit on top of the table. Oaks was startled and wanted to run but remained still and silent. They would order the guard to take a hand off if he were caught stealing from them. He watched as the guard walked from around the table and headed away.

"Nora, help me take the fish to the back," a young lady said to another.

Oaks watched as they carried the nets around the corner. Another girl took the buckets with shells and followed behind. Another young girl the age of no more than six came around the table toward her grandmother and said, "I wanted to show Papa all the shells I found."

"He will be back, and you can show him then. I know he will love everything you found," her grandmother replied. "Let's get them cleaned up. I will show you how to make a necklace."

The girl and her grandmother took the bucket off the table. Oaks saw their feet turn the other direction and darted out from the table and under the next set of tables without being seen. He moved quicker among the tables until he reached the end. He peaked through the hanging cloths toward the alley, looking to see if the way was clear. Out from under the last table and into the small alleyway, he took off.

Into the darkened doorway, he hid against the wall. Breathing heavy, Oaks turned back to look in each direction. He waited for a few moments checking to see if anyone had followed him. No one was around and made their way into that alleyway. As he entered the dark niche, Oaks whispered for his sister, "Tessa? Are you still in here?"

"Yes," she replied, standing to her feet. "I'm shivering."

"Here, something for you to change into," Oaks said. He handed her a few garments bunched together.

"You were gone for a while," she said reaching out to take them. "Here's your sword back. I thought you weren't coming back."

"I had to hide until the guards left. They were taking someone to Father. I heard them say that he was requesting the villagers come and see him."

"Turn around and make sure no one comes in here while I change. I'm cold and need to get warm," Tessa said. She stepped back to the darkened corner. "My fingers have turned numb. They are probably purple now."

"Just try to hurry, we need to be ready to run," he replied, and checked the alleyway again.

Tessa stepped out of her wet clothes and tossed them over to the other corner. She slid dark garments on. The sleeves covered her arms as she had wanted. Impressed, she was happy that Oaks had thought of everything for her. *It's nice to slide my feet into a pair of dry shoes,* she thought as she tightened the straps across the top. She took a string and pulled her hair back while walking to the entry way next to her brother, she asked, "Do you have a plan of how we are going to get out of here?"

"Yes, it's the same way Isidore took me and Seiji without being noticed," he replied.

"Are you sure that we have to leave?" she asked, peaking the other way down the alley. "You don't think we can speak with Father?"

"I'm leaving, but if you want to stay… then go back home. I know what I saw, and Father is not the same. According to what you saw, Mother isn't right either. If you are coming with me this is your chance. So, what is it going to be?"

"I…" she replied, sounding hesitant and thought about going back home to herself. "Alright, I'm coming with you."

"Then take this. I stole it for you too," he said.

"Thank you," she replied.

She looked down. It was a strap that held a small dagger. Her soft hands took hold of the belt as she fastened it around her waist. She snapped the buttons and unsheathed the knife looking at its curved blade.

She went to touch the blade, but Oaks stopped her and said, "Don't touch that part, you will lose a finger. Or whatever that part touches will be cut. When we get beyond these walls it will be dangerous. If anything, or anyone touches you, I want you to stab it and don't hesitate. You may not get another chance to do so."

"Where do I need to stab it?" she asked.

"Right here," he replied and lifted the blade to his throat. "This is where Barron showed me to strike, and that's what Father did to him."

"Are you serious?" she asked.

"Of course, I'm not making it up," he replied and turned her hand with the dagger down. "Keep it sheathed for now. Darkness will soon be here. And when it is, we will make our way. I will keep a lookout in this direction, you can keep watch the other way."

"And if I see the guards?"

"If they are coming this way... We run."

"Hopefully, they won't catch us," she replied and looked toward the end of the alleyway.

The sky turned a dark blue with orange streaks stretched across its vastness as the sun faded. The wind continued to blow and whistle throughout Fog-shore as it did often. Walls of the alleyway soon blended with the dimness as they both kept watch for any guards. Villagers began lighting torches around their shops as those who enjoyed the night life ventured out. Oaks took Tessa by the arm and said, "Come on, this way and stay close and copy everything that I do."

"What about food?" she asked. The smell of cooking made her stomach growl. "What are we going to eat?"

"I stole food and blankets earlier, and more the last time I went out," he replied, grabbing his bag. "Now keep up."

"So, you thought of everything?" she asked.

"Ssh," he hushed her. "Save your questions for when we are away from here."

"Alright, I'm just getting…"

"Ssh," he hushed her again.

"Hungry," she said with a hushed tone.

"I will give you something, but we have to go now, quietly."

"I get it," she replied with a soft tone.

Down the alleyway and away from the shops, they went toward the darker and narrow stonewalls that led to the wooden docks. As they eased along the wall, Tessa followed Oaks. Once they reached the end, he stopped and pulled Tessa's sleeve to crouch. Around the corner, his face slightly peaked to see if the way was clear. With a gentle tug, he grabbed Tessa's hand, he whispered, "This way."

Across the sand and to a set of wooden stairs, they went up and followed the docks that took them out and over the water. Behind a wall of one of the houses, they squatted down as a few villagers passed by. Once they were gone, Oaks looked to make sure no one else was around and led them to a house. Tied to the docks, small boats knocked against the wooden planks. Oaks dropped down into one of them, he turned and helped his sister to get in. Tessa grabbed the sides to hang on for the little boat was quite shaky. Oaks pulled out his dagger and cut the rope freeing them. Under the docks, they disappeared as he rowed with soft strokes. To the main gate, they both headed on. It led out to sea, but he stopped at the docks end as large ships entered and left. Tessa helped him steady their small boat by hanging on one of the docks wooden braces. The waves lifted and rocked them as she knelt and steadied herself to push them off. A perfect opportunity to cross through the choppy waters was what he looked for or they could be crushed by those entering and exiting. Looking over his shoulder, he spoke with a soft tone to Tessa saying, "Now."

She pushed them underway and out from underneath the docks. In between the large ships, Oaks rowed softly, not to make too much noise as they made their approach to the stonewall that surrounded Fog-shore. There he rowed along the edge without being noticed or in harm's way. Through the gate, along eastern wall, and to the shoreline, Tessa and Oaks left their Fathers kingdom.

CHAPTER

8

" **O**llie, my friend..." Bralgon said, with his arms out giving Ollie a hug. "I have some new digging tools I brought with me to give to you and Cora. My gift to you."

"Those are nice, thank you," Ollie said, picking up the stone pick.

"You're welcome," Bralgon said, popping Ollie in the arm almost making him drop the stone pick.

"Ouch," Ollie grunted.

"Don't tell me marriage has already made you soft, now? Are you going to be able to dig?"

"Yes," he replied.

"Yes, marriage has made you soft?" Bralgon asked and smiled with a half grin.

"No, marriage hasn't made me soft," Ollie replied

GARRIS L. R. COLEMAN

and turning the stone pick over in his hand.

"What are you grunting at then?"

"Ah nothing at all, only a heavy stone pick in my hand," Ollie said. He placed it over his shoulder.

They both turned as a door closed behind them. It was Cora coming out of the bedroom, as she lifted her hair off her neck and tied it with a ribbon. With a smile on her face she said, "Okay... I'm all sorted and ready to go."

"Look, Bralgon brought some new digging tools for us."

"Nice, thank you Bralgon," Cora said. "You're too kind."

"You're welcome, Love."

"So... are we ready to go?" Cora asked.

"I'm ready. Are you ready, Bralgon?" Ollie asked.

"After you... my friend," Bralgon replied, picking up his stone pick and walking over to the door.

"Do you remember how to get there, Cora?" Ollie asked as they began to leave their home.

"Of course, I do. What sort of question is that?"

"Okay, good, we will follow you then," Ollie said.

"So, how was Kettle Island?" Bralgon asked, while they were walking on their way to the dig site.

"It was beautiful."

"Of course, it was beautiful… tell me a little more."

"We sailed on a ship to get there. The water was

clear with a light blue tint. The sand was a brilliant bright white and you could hear the ocean waves crashing onto the shore as we slept. It was amazing. We got to watch the sun go down every night from our room. There were huge trees everywhere and all kinds of unique creatures. I wish we could go back. It was like an undiscovered land," Ollie said, thinking back on the great time they had.

"Sounds quite amazing," Bralgon replied.

"That's because it is... you need to hurry up and get married so you can go. It's something wonderful to see and experience," Ollie said, encouraging him.

"You know me. I probably will never marry; I like them all."

"Surely there's one that can tame the wild Bralgon?" Cora said, looking back over her shoulder.

"I actually have met someone... if I was thinking of marrying, she probably would be one I would choose."

"That's marvelous," Cora said with excitement.

"Yeah... that is excellent," Ollie said.

"Are you going to give us a name?" Cora asked.

"Her name is Ashlin."

"Ashlin... sounds like a nice name," Ollie said.

"When do we get to meet her?" Cora asked.

"Wait, I didn't say I was going to marry her, I only

said she would make a good one to marry."

"That's okay, we wouldn't say anything to Ashlin. We just would like to meet her, is all," Cora said, offering friendly support to Bralgon.

"We will stand by whatever your choice you make," Ollie said, agreeing with Cora.

"There's the dig site," Cora said, pointing over to the mountain's side.

Noticing an odd stone sticking out of the side, Cora took her stone pick and began striking at it. With the stone crumbling, she found a large Dahlia gem.

"Wow, that is huge," Bralgon said as he was impressed with her first find of the day.

"Just pick a spot and dig," Cora said, leaning over to pick up her gem.

"You heard the lady," Ollie said, teasing with Bralgon.

"I will be over there near the rocks," Cora said.

"We might need to dig where she's digging," Bralgon said.

"You can dig where I'm going to be," Cora said.

"Okay, let's go," Bralgon said, as they followed Cora to the area where there were more stones.

"I think it would great if you got married to Ashlin," Ollie said swinging his chisel into the stone.

"So, we're back on that?" Bralgon asked, cracking a stone with his stone pick.

"I would be very happy for you, is all that I'm saying."

"Oh, look, I found one," Bralgon said, picking up the gem and handing it to Ollie.

"Don't keep pressuring him about getting married," Cora said, swinging her digging tool.

"You heard the lady," Bralgon said, teasing Ollie.

"Okay… I won't say anything else about it," Ollie answered, just as all three of them swung their tools into the stone at once.

With all three of them hitting the stone, there was something different. The mountain rumbled as if it answered back. They pulled out the picks as the stones began to crumble, and the rocks went tumbling down the side. They jumped to the side. Bralgon grabbed Ollie, pulling him out of the way of falling rocks. A cloud of dust from all the rubble filled the air causing Cora to be obscured from them.

"CORA!" Ollie shouted, calling out to her. He shouted again for her, "CORA!"

"I'm okay," Cora shouted back as her voice sounded tiny because it was in the distance, for she had slid down the mountainside, avoiding some of the rocks that had fallen.

"I'm coming to you," Ollie shouted, then started climbing down toward her.

Loose rubble slid as Cora reached toward a stone

bulging from the cliff. She ducked to avoid more rocks hitting her. Each time she tried to climb up the side of the mountain, more debris fell trapping her. Ollie and Bralgon began making their way to her. On the ledge they both reached down as she stretched out her hands. They easily pulled her up onto the ledge where they were. She stood to her feet and brushed herself off. Cora's hair and clothing were covered with the mountain's dust and debris.

"Are you alright?" Ollie asked.

"Yes, I'm fine," Cora said, hugging Ollie.

"What was that?" Cora asked.

"I don't know, I've never seen that happen before," Bralgon answered.

"Me neither," Ollie said.

"Look, it's like the mountain opened," Cora said while pointing up.

They stood staring at the gaping rupture in the mountain's side. Bralgon reached out and took hold of the protruding rocks and started to climb. Cora and Ollie followed making their way back to the top where they had been. Once reaching the top, they stood and looked below them and realized how much of the mountain had split and was open. Astonished at what was before them, they were not sure of what had just happened.

"Did you see that?" Ollie asked.

"See what?" Bralgon asked.

"There was a light that flickered," Ollie said, gazing down into the abyss.

"A light?" Bralgon asked.

"There it was again!" Ollie said.

"I saw it too, that time," Cora said, taking a bold step into the darkness to satisfy her curiosity.

"What are you doing?" Ollie asked.

"I'm going inside," Cora said, starting to climb over a rock.

"No, I will go first," Ollie said, as he began leading the way down into the abyss.

"Watch your step," Ollie said, helping Cora.

"Where do you think it leads?" Bralgon asked, walking cautiously while looking at the walls.

"I don't know," Ollie said, just as they came around the bending of the tunnel.

They followed a purple glow reflecting in the dim light, its shimmer danced upon the walls and brought their attention closer to a sphere. They stood amazed and astonished, the light flickered and was drawing them in.

"Is that a gem?" Cora asked, while whispering.

"I don't know," Bralgon answered.

"Yeah, I was about to ask the same thing," Ollie said.

"It sure is beautiful," Cora said, fascinated by it.

She wanted to reach out and touch it.

Its brightness projected a glistening light. It was lustrous and enticing. The light was small and offered great pleasure to the eye.

With hearing the rolling of rubble approaching them, they looked down and saw something emerging from the corner. The dark figure stepped out of the shadow. Bralgon and Cora stepped back as Ollie knelt on his knee to take a closer look, for what he saw was only one-fourth of his size and never had been seen before.

*"Sshá él são kōō **ná**,"* the witch uttered with a venomous tone.

"What are you?" Ollie asked, leaning over trying to speak with it.

While looking into its face, Ollie only saw an eye staring back at him, blinking when he blinked. A voice came forth from the witch as it began to move and speak again, turning from the wall, carefully, not to spook them.

"I am desire, devotion, and delight," the witch answered.

Away from the walls and rising, the witch began to rotate slowly, growing and becoming the same size as the Tavorians right before their eyes. The walls vibrated and expanded. Even the reflecting purple shimmer grew with the witch. As the witch grew, Ollie began to see more than an eye, his whole reflection became apparent in the witch's face. With one swipe of its hand into the purple glowing light, the witch opened its hand and held three gems - one for each of them.

"Take them… a gift from the Lord of all," the witch said, seeing their deep desire for gems of all sorts.

"Who is Lord of all?" Ollie asked, staring at the gems feeling a heavy force swaying him to take hold them.

"His name is Lord Sicarius."

"Lord Sicarius?"

"Yes..." The witch said, holding out its other hand showing all the universe rotating and every world within it and their types of gems. "All of these hidden treasures and more will be yours," the witch said, enticing them.

"We can have all of these treasures?" Cora asked.

"Yes, all of them starting with these," the witch said, extending its hand further.

"Why does he want to give them to us?" Bralgon asked.

"His Majesty is gracious and shares his kingdom with all, but if you don't want them, I will tell him you didn't like his gems," the witch said, pulling back its hand with the gems in it.

"Wait," Bralgon said, while the witch was placing visions in each of their minds. "I will take a gem, I never said I didn't want one," Bralgon said, reaching out and taking hold of it.

"You are in favor with King Sicarius now," the witch said, as Bralgon stared into the gem he held.

"I would like to have one also," Cora said, reaching out her hand to take a gem from the witch, especially after seeing that nothing happened to Bralgon when he took a gem.

"You're going to take the gem too?" Ollie asked.

"Yes, it's a gift," Cora said, receiving the gem.

"You will be named Delight before his Majesty," the witch said, as Cora stared into the gem that she held.

"Ah, last, but not least, this one is yours. All you have to do is accept it."

"What will happen if I don't accept?" Ollie asked.

"Nothing. This is as far as I can go into your world," the witch said.

"And if I do accept, what will happen?"

"You may go, to any of these worlds and the gems will be yours."

"Any of these worlds?" Ollie asked.

"Yes… all of them if you wish. Look closer and you will have a foretaste of all the riches that are to come," the witch said, showing him a vision.

Cora was wearing a provocative garment, decorated with all types of gems from the other worlds. She grabbed his hand and pulled, inviting him to follow her, but it was the witch's power that was pulling at him as his hand inched closer and closer to taking the gem.

"Where did she go?" Ollie asked, seeing that Cora had disappeared in his vision.

"Just show your devotion to your spouse and it is yours," the witch said, continuing its pull on Ollie.

The witch whispered only to Ollie, while he was having a vision of Cora reappearing, enticing, and pulling him toward her. She took him into her kingdom where there were gems, gold, and all sorts of precious stones. He stretched his hand forward wanting to give in to his desire. Ollie paused as his fingertips touched the gem softly. It was cool to the skin, so he took hold of the gem.

With Bralgon's choice of taking the last gem, it unlocked the power of the three jewels. A fog released quickly into the air spraying Bralgon, Cora, and Ollie in their faces, causing them to inhale the gems mist, enticing them even more.

"Go and bring all of your kind to me so that they too may also share in the riches of all the new worlds. I will show your people what is in your hand when the time is right. Go to where there are many around," the witch commanded.

Bralgon, Cora, and Ollie turned in unison and went to the mouth of the cavern and left with their new gems.

CHAPTER
9

Clank clank, the sounds of footsteps resonated throughout the long hall. A guard approached at the end of the entryway. Scuffing against the floor, he stopped, and echoes of his feet subsided. Grabbing hold of the handles, he pulled opened two tall bulky doors. They were mahogany stained reaching halfway to the ceiling with carvings of winding tree limbs intricately entangled behind a single shield and double swords crossing each other. The thick doors provided a sound barrier and led into a reserved room off the hallway before reaching The Great Echo Hall. Walking through the entrance, the guard entered, and the councilmen turned their attention. While looking at him, they became silent and some stood to their feet.

"My Lords, King Elias is now ready for you all," Kiros said, to the councilmen who were waiting to resume their meeting.

Sliding their chairs back, many of them murmured unpleasant things amongst themselves while clearing out of the room. Down the long hallway, the councilmen followed Kiros into The Great Echo Hall through another set of bulky doors with the same carvings as the others. Guards lined each side of the walls holding spears in an upright position while the guards closest to the King and Queen held their hands on the hilt of sheathed swords, awaiting any given commands to obey. King Elias sat on his newly acclaimed throne, watching them enter, with Queen Sienna by his side.

"What is the meaning of all this?" asked the councilman Hiram, while stepping over puddles of blood covering the floor.

"All those who oppose us... will die," King Elias replied.

"Have you gone mad?" Hiram asked. He and the other councilmen had grown agitated, having waited for Elias to return. He saw their plans and the table and papers destroyed and his chair stolen by the Queen. His face tightened almost to a frown now seeing the ends of his golden-brown clothing stained. He could not keep it from dragging across the floor and out of the blood.

"Ha-ha-ha," Queen Sienna laughed. "Have you gone mad... ha-ha-ha... Have you gone mad, he asks," the Queen said, repeating him. She stood to her feet and looked over at the King.

She took a step away from her throne and lifted the bottom edges of her dress while she made her way down each of the steps. She walked toward Hiram and began to encircle him. Her hand slid across the back of his shoulders, she stopped and stood in front of him asked, "Should we rip out his tongue?"

"My Lady," Hiram said, with an apologetic tone, widening his eyes.

"I know..." she said, grabbing his face and leaning in toward him, "I will teach you how to speak. Seems it would be fitting since you are the appointed speaker for the council," Queen Sienna said. She tilted her head, opening her mouth and using her tongue, it turned into the form of a snake and entered through Hiram's mouth causing him to convulse.

Kiros slammed the doors behind them, trapping all the councilmen inside The Great Echo Hall. They looked over at the door as it slammed, startling them. King Elias stood to his feet. He made his way down each step. Some of the councilmen backed away while many of the others stood in place before King Elias.

"New trading has begun. Join us and keep your

life, or choose to oppose us and die," King Elias said, offering them a chance to keep their lives.

"My Lord, we have never opposed you," Old Man Fish said. He was one the ones who bowed his head before King Elias, followed by several of his fellow councilmen.

"My Lord?" King Elias said, repeating Old Man Fish. "I am now, Your Grace," King Elias corrected him. "You all are lords because I allow you to own a small piece of land, but I own everything."

"Yes, Your Grace," Old Man Fish replied, nodding his head, then looking over toward the thud that was made. Hiram's body fell to the floor and lay motionless after the Queen pulled away from him.

"Ah, he will live," Queen Sienna said, turning her focus to the other councilmen.

"I know of your plans, your plots, and the words that you bicker amongst yourselves. I have seen into the future and what outcome you think will happen to me and my family," King Elias said. His hand was behind his back. "I also know of the coin given to Barron to betray me if I were not to implement its value."

"I want no part in any of this, Your Grace," Councilman Mason said stepping forward.

"But you have a part in this and have set in motion things that can't be undone."

"No, Your Grace," he replied.

"If my memory serves me correctly, it was you who brought to my attention that I would be rewarded handsomely. Was it not? And now you want to leave?"

"Yes, Your Grace. I only want to leave. I gave coin to Barron to only help in persuading you and for him to introduce it."

"I tell you," King Elias said, placing his hands-on Mason's shoulders. "I don't need persuading. I'm all for the coin. You may leave. Go with the Kings blessings."

"Thank you, Your Grace," Mason bowed his head and turned to leave. He took a step as a point covered in red protruded from his chest, dripping. The big man fell to his knees, Elias stood over him and leaned closer to him.

"Don't forget your parting gift," King Elias said, pulling the sword away. He walked in front of Mason and looked down at him. "I know you think many of the men belong to you, but that's all going to change very soon."

Mason held his chest and found it difficult to breathe. Blood gushed through his chubby fingers as he looked up and saw Elias. The new king swung his blade and sliced opened his throat. One of the guards that belonged to Mason eased toward the door. He was standing near the back and lifted the handle to push the door open. Going unnoticed after seeing Mason killed, he slipped out of the doorway.

"Would anyone else like to leave with the Kings' blessing?"

"No, Your Grace," Old Man Fish said and eased down to his knees.

The other councilmen followed Old Man Fish's lead and knelt before King Elias. All their attention turned to the Queen as they heard her make another rattling sound. She stepped away from Hiram as he remained lying on the stone floor. Queen Sienna slightly lifted her dress, walked over and stood behind Old Man Fish. Grabbing the side of his face, she leaned his head back on to her chest. Looking up at the queen, his eyes widened with concern.

"My Lady," he said, with fear in his voice.

"I am now, Your Majesty," Queen Sienna said, correcting them.

"Yes, of course, my apologies Your Majesty," he replied, looking up at the Queen.

"It's good you have never opposed us," she said. "You will learn about plotting against Your King and Queen."

"I have Never plotted against either of you, Your Majesty."

"Well then, you won't mind if I do this," Queen Sienna said, gripping the side of his face harder.

Her eyes darkened as two white slits flashed across the middle. Old Man Fish stared into her eyes as she opened her mouth and her tongue made a rattle.

"AH!" Old Man Fish let out a grunt.

CHAPTER
10

*R*idged stones rolled down the mountain side as the Tavorians reached up and onto rocks to lift themselves out. Ollie, Cora, and Bralgon made their way away from the cave. Through the tree line and soft grassy trails, they made their way to the stone paths that would direct them toward the crowds. The three approached the alleyways and stairs that led to the top of Mount Ouranos. Ollie, Cora, and Bralgon went to where there would be many Tavorians gathered. The evening was near and that was when they knew most of their feasting took place.

The sound of laughter and celebration filled the air as they came closer and arrived at the stone arches. They each went separate ways, the three made their way past the open yards of onyx stones. The dark-green stones were in the shape of ovals and shimmered against the marble stone walls. Bralgon made his way toward Crog Tavern, where stone tossing took place. As he entered the Tavern, a friend of his saw him and said, "Bralgon, they're trying to beat your record." But he just walked past his friend without saying anything. The friend had tightened his eyebrows as a concerned look came over his face, he thought it was strange that Bralgon did not reply. The Tavorian walked after him calling his name, "Bralgon are you alright? You seem different... Bralgon?" he continued until he grabbed his arm to stop him. "Bralgon?"

Bralgon stopped and turned toward his friend and lifted his hand. With a slow turn of his fist his fingers faced upward and, he said, "A gift from the king."

"A what?" the Tavorian asked, he turned his head slightly to an angle. He looked at Bralgon as if he had lost his mind.

The Tavorian's eyes glanced down at Bralgon's clinched fist. His hand began to lose color with his tight grip. It was pale as the veins running up his arm were even more discolored. Confused, the Tavorian Tavern keeper raised an eyebrow as each of Bralgon's fingers began to slowly open. A mist blew into the keeper's face and filled the air around them.

Cora went toward the Tavorians that were from the Ruby Shores. In Argon it was known that those who came from there to visit Mount Oranous brought a special red ruby with them. Many Tavorians traveled from the southern lands with carts filled to the brim. The Tavorians could drink from these rubies. The darker the rubies were the sweeter they tasted. Sweeter than any wine made from grapes or plums. On the Ruby Shores was where Cora lived most of her life until she and her parents moved onto Mount Oranous. It was not long after their move that she had met Ollie. Most of her family members remained living in the south. Everyone that was from Ruby Shores were her relatives. Her family had a strong influence on that part of Argon's region and loved to visit Mount Oranous frequently.

Cora stood motionless amongst her people as they were sharing their rubies and conversing. She kept her head looking down and her hand clenched at her side. Many Tavorians did not pay attention to her as they continued walking around on either side. But one of the Tavorians accidently bumped into her shoulder and dropped a few rubies and said, "I'm sorry." She paused as she looked up at Cora and continued speaking, "Good to see you again, Cora." the Tavorian, had recognized her. It was one of her relatives. Cora remained looking down, staring at her clinched fist. Her cousin placed a hand on Cora's arm. "Cora, are you alright? You seem different."

Cora raised her hand and turned her palm over the same way Bralgon had done and said, "A gift from the king."

Her cousin looked down as she opened her hand. A mist sprayed from the jewel and into the air. It surrounded them and was gone as quickly as it appeared.

Another union before the crown elite had begun to take place and the sun was setting in the background. Most of the Tavorians who came to make their vows preferred to express their love toward each other that way. They called their sun Amber. And they believed that the sun took the exchange of the lovers' words and stored them with the stars. Many called them, the Moments of Amber's-promise.

A couple were in the middle of having the strands that dispersed into the water tied around their wrists when Ollie walked and stood in front of the crowd. They all turned their eyes to him. The fathers stopped what they were doing. Their faces cut toward each other and stopped talking. He raised his arm midway to open his hand but stopped. The shining and flickering of the crown elite caught his eye. He turned his head to the side and went along the stone pathway. All the Tavorians that were there watched as he approached stepping in between the couple's fathers. He almost knocked the couple out of the way as he went and stood near the fount of The Crown Elite. One of the Tavorians turned and asked, "May we help you with something?"

Ollie lifted his arm again about midway out and replied, "A gift from the King."

Many of the Tavorians were confused as Ollie opened his hand. The mist filled the air all around them. The gem slid out of his palm as he turned it over dumping it into the water. The Tavorian couple stepped back and apart from each other as their strand broke and fell to the ground.

Controlled by the witch, their opened hand revealed the gem to everyone that was near regardless of who they were. The friends and family had no understanding of what was happening. Bralgon, Cora, and Ollie carried the gems that they had brought back from the witch to a special location.

The three locations were chosen because most of the Tavorian population stayed in those areas. Ollie, Cora, and Bralgon were blinded in their minds by the vapor from earlier. All three of them kept their hands open and level the same way, allowing the gems to begin spraying a mist amongst the Tavorians. They had no awareness that they were spreading the mist among the others. Soon, the mist surrounded many of the Tavorians, making them easily convinced of wanting gems from other worlds. Compelled, Ollie grabbed The Crown Elite on either side. He took a deep breath, used all his strength, and lifted The Crown Elite, breaking it free from its pillar, placing it upon his head.

CHAPTER

11

A **small** group of Hurons that had gathered grew impatient and restless while family members and friends stood outside the Pagoda. Many of the Hurons returned to the Pagoda and stood outside the doors looking to Taiki for guidance. The Hurons wanted Elias to be held responsible for his actions. A voice speaking above the crowd was upset and had many Huron's angered. He walked and bumped shoulders with them while making his way toward the front to where Taiki was.

"My brother, Cai, is dead. Elias needs to answer for what he has done," Brax claimed. Tension increased as the crowd became angrier.

"Before there is any more bloodshed, we need to understand more of what's going on," Zalm said, addressing the crowd.

"I will tell you what's going on," Brax said, walking in front of Zalm, standing close to his face. "Elias murdered my brother along with other innocent from our village. He is to make all of us his slaves, or even kill us if we don't bow to him."

"Brax, my brother, I'm not your enemy," Zalm said.

"Nor am I your enemy. This is an act of war, brother," Brax said.

"Brax is right," Taiki said, the crowd became silent wanting to hear him speak. "My son... our family members were murdered a few days ago, this is an act of war. If Elias thinks he can murder as he pleases, then he needs to be stopped. Anyone who wants to leave may do so, now."

Everyone became silent and eyes looked around the Pagoda, Taiki made eye contact with several of the men waiting to see who was going to leave. Many turned and looked at each other as the villagers mumbled amongst themselves before turning their attention back to Taiki.

"I see that no one is leaving. Good. We will make Elias surrender and answer for his crimes. If he doesn't, then we will burn his village down and everyone along with it. If a war is what Elias wants... then war it is," Taiki said. Horns began to sound in the distance outside of Huron Village.

"Those are not our horns, Sir," Zalm said, as horns started to sound near them.

"Now, those are ours," Taiki said, as a different sound was heard.

"To your positions!" Someone shouted from the chaos.

The blaring of war horns kept sounding from the distance. The men of Huron village began to scramble, exiting the Pagoda, grabbing swords, and readying themselves for whatever was upon them. As they got closer to the fence and, they saw that Elias already had his men march halfway around Huron Village, and they were ready to attack Huron Village. Lined up, waiting for Elias to give the orders to attack, they stood with spears and swords in hand.

Taiki and Zalm stood at the gate looking out from the gaps. Several Hurons lined up next to each other ready to face the threat. Many of them scrambled and rushed to hide their families. Taiki looked over at Zalm and said, "I will try to give our people more time to hide and get ready.

"We have arrived at war a lot sooner than we expected," Zalm replied.

"Agreed, much sooner than I'm ready for," Taiki said and climbed up on his horse. "Open the gate."

"I will come with you," Zalm said as he climbed on a horse also. A few men rode with them on horses to meet Elias.

Silver amour sparkled in the sun as Taiki and his men stopped several feet from the guards. Tall winter grasses swayed in the fields and rustled as they brushed up against one another. The horses snorted and turned in place. Elias walked out from among his guards and met them. He stood with guards on either side of him and said, "I take it you received my 'gift'?"

"Gift? Why would you commit such atrocity? I thought you and I were friends?" Taiki asked.

"Things are changing…" Elias replied.

"Did you come to surrender and answer for your crimes?" Taiki asked.

"Did you come to bow to your new king?" Elias replied, firmly.

"King… you are not my king," Taiki said, in a harsh tone. "You are nothing more than a murderer and I will accept nothing but your complete surrender."

"Look around Taiki… we outnumber you," Elias said, with arrogance.

"You must answer for your crimes," Taiki said.

"You're not thinking clearly, Taiki. Think of your men and their families. Bow to me… I will let you all live."

"I'd rather die than bow to you," Taiki said, turning away.

"I will be sure to make it a painful death for you,"

Elias said, watching Taiki and his men turn and make their way back to their village.

"Your Grace, shall we begin?" Kiros asked.

"Bring Taiki to me... alive," Elias said, sitting in a chair wearing a thick, grayish, wool coat made from an animal hide that came down to his knees. "Oh, let's give them the rest of their 'gifts'."

"Yes, Your Grace," Kiros replied.

Kiros did as the king commanded, loading the 'gifts' and had them catapulted into the village, hoping to instill fear into the Huron Village. Latches released and ropes unwound, sending wooden arms shooting upward, they used the headless bodies of Cai and his men as a ballista. Through the air they went flying and flailing, bodies hit some of the Huron villagers and crashed into their homes, but this intimidation tactic failed, only making the Hurons more furious. For Taiki, this caused him concern for Misaki and her safety. He looked behind and saw Misaki outside of the Pagoda. Taiki rode over to her and climbed down from his horse.

"Here, take the horse, get Oma and leave. Elias is here, and we are outnumbered," Taiki said.

"Come with us," Misaki said.

"I can't, the men and everyone here are looking to me for guidance and they are ready for this war. There's no stopping them now. I won't leave them behind. You don't have much time. Go... get far away from here. As far as you can," Taiki said.

This time, another loud eerie horn sounded. It was Elias calling The Cursed to march with his men upon Huron Village.

"GO!" Taiki shouted, forcing Misaki to leave, then running off to fight alongside his men. "Hold the line," Taiki shouted, commanding his men.

Misaki rode over to where her mother was and entered the room with haste. The door swung opened. She grabbed her mother by the hand. She tried to pull her out of the room to leave, but Oma snatched her hand down to her side.

"Mother, we must go," Misaki said, making it out of the door.

"Wait, help me get Higotji," Oma said, stopping Misaki.

"Mother, leave him, we have no time, people are running to the forest to hide. Elias is here."

"Then just go with them," Oma said.

"No... I'm not leaving you."

"I can just hide somewhere."

"Okay, I will help you with him, but we must hurry," Misaki said, turning back to get him.

Higotji eased out from the bed with an arm around Misaki's neck. Her mother had given him a powerful medicine before they were under replied. It had made him relaxed and too weak to stand own his own. They made their way outside to a wooden wagon where the horse was hitched to it. Higotji, tried to climb as Misaki and Oma helped him up as chaos began to unfold around them. Many of the Hurons ran for their lives to find places to hide, while many of the villagers fought to save their people. Children looked for small places to crawl inside, while others fled to the nearby forest in hope of escaping. It was not long before Huron Village's wooden fence was trampled as it was broken and torn down. Elias's men entered Huron Village with The Cursed alongside them. Like a pack of wild and vicious animals, they chased after the villagers. The savage creatures managed to catch many of the Huron people. They sunk their claws and teeth into their skin and violently shook their heads tearing the flesh open.

Off in the distance, the crashing sound of metal rang out as steel collided against steel. The men grunted as blades slid across armor and the edge side found its way into an opening to cut flesh. The shouts from the men made Misaki look toward the front gates to see if she could see her husband.

"Here, climb up, Mother. Take him. I will find another horse. I'll catch up with you, now go," Misaki said.

"I don't want to leave you," Oma said.

"Just go. There's no time. I will get that horse over there, now go," Misaki said, running toward the other horse.

They rode toward the back side of Huron Village as The Cursed chased after Oma and Higotji trying to cut them off. Stretched arms and claws flung out as foul creatures jumped trying to catch them. Oma steered the horse with a quick turn, making one of The Cursed miss its target. It rolled into another Cursed and they knocked each other away allowing Oma and Higotji to escape from Huron Village through the back gate. Through trees and up a hill, they put a great distance between them and their village. Oma and Higotji rode to the top of a small ridge that overlooked their home. They stopped and turned back to face their village. The horse took a few steps as if it wanted to continue forward. It snorted as they looked to see if they could see any of the chaos.

"No… stop!" Oma said, crying out, wanting Elias to cease attacking her village. "I shouldn't have left."

"I'm sorry this is happening Oma," Higotji said, holding his chest.

"My people," Oma said, stretching out her hand for them.

"Oma, do you hear that?" Higotji asked, pointing toward the rattling of leaves in the forest. "Something is coming... over there."

Over in the tree line, a horse snorted as it emerged from amongst the greenery. The tree limbs rustled and bent downward as a hand pushed the branches out of the way. It was Misaki catching up to them. Sweat and the dark color of blood ran down her neck and covered sections of her clothing. Saddened for her people, Oma had a moment of relief, seeing her daughter.

"Oh, my daughter... are you okay? Oma asked, reaching out to Misaki as she rode up next to her. "Are you bleeding?"

"I'm okay, it's not my blood. Don't watch this horror Mother, we must keep riding. Here, take these, looks like we're going to need them," Misaki said, handing Oma and Higotji swords.

"These swords aren't the ones we make," Oma said, noticing something different while taking a sword.

"No... I took them from the soldiers I killed before leaving the village. I killed two of the *Má Baé* that were chasing you. Come, Mother, let's go."

CHAPTER
12

The men and women of Huron village who stayed behind fought ferociously but were outnumbered. Alongside Elias's men, The Cursed came into the village at the command of the sound of a horn. The vile creature's bit and scratched at everything that lived. Some feed on the fallen corpses of Elias's dead guards and the bodies of the Huron Villagers. Anything living or dead was not safe from them. The living feared their attacks as much as death itself. For when the *Má Baé* sank their claws and teeth into flesh, the mark began the curse.

All around the fields of Huron Village swords swung and clashed against metal and wooden spears. The sound was muffled along with the cries and screams of those around. The eyes of dead corpses remained opened as their bodies laid motionless and blood staining the grasses. A twitch from a body limb moved as more of the Huron's fought. The sounds of fighting became louder as bodies from the fallen on both sides sat up. Their eyes were sunk inward, the teeth were sharp and claws ready for slashing. Onto their feet running, The Cursed did not have to wait long before making their attack. The newly *Má Baé* ran toward the closest living or dead thing to attack. Their blood was contagious and even known to wake the dead. The Huron's continued fighting as the dead corpses in the grasses stood infected.

Overrun with The Cursed and King Elias's guards, Huron Village fell. Elias lifted his horn and blew once more, and the vile creatures scattered in all directions. Over the broken fence and into the woods they went as fast they came. Taiki and several of his men were surrounded by Elias's soldiers. With several hundred spears pointing at them, they were forced to surrender. Elias commanded his soldiers to gather the survivors and had them brought before him. With his hand on his hilt and approaching King Elias, Kiros said, "We have the survivors, Your Grace."

"Lock them in chains and make sure Taiki is separated from the others. I have something special for him. And…" he paused, looking down at his horn, then raising his head, "Bring Taiki to me," King Elias commanded.

"Yes, Your Grace."

Arms stretched out and chained to a board that was notched to fit around his neck, Taiki's ankles were chained together just wide enough to make a step. Many of the villagers tried to see through to the captives, but the guards blocked them. The Huron Villagers were kept separate and Taiki was led away from his people. A short stick was poked into his back over and over with a thrusting force that propelled him forward. Kiros brought Taiki before King Elias and with a hard push to his back, forced Taiki to the ground on his knees. Clothes torn, sweating, and breathing heavily, Taiki's black stringy hair was messy from fighting and hung down covering most of his face but with one eye showing.

"I told you... bow and you all would live. Now, look at you, ended up on your knees anyway, and your people... you chose to lose everything," Elias said, walking closer and standing before Taiki.

King Elias exhaled and shook his head as he came even closer and began speaking again. Taiki used what little strength he had by taking his right arm, chained to the board, he swung his arm around, hitting the back of Elias's leg, sweeping him off his feet. Dirt flung up and the chains rattled as Elias landed on his back. Taiki began hitting him swiftly with the end of the board and landed a strike to his mouth. Taiki wanted desperately to finish this by attempting to bash Elias's head. The guards quickly intervened. Two of the guards grabbed Taiki and slung him onto his back. Standing over him, they unsheathed their swords, ready to stab him.

"WAIT!" Elias shouted. Rolling over onto his hands and knees, spitting blood, he reached into his pocket and pulled out a cloth. Wiping his mouth, he stood with a grin upon his face. "Ha-ha..." Elias laughed, thinking the attack was humorous.

"Your Grace, shall I kill him?" Kiros asked.

"Get him up," Elias commanded. "Before we leave... you will see, and blood you will taste," he said, standing face to face with Taiki while the guards held him in place this time.

"You are nothing more than a murderer," Taiki said, spitting into Elias's face.

"Yes, I am... and you have no idea," Elias said, spitting blood back into Taiki's face. "Now, bring all of the children, here," Elias commanded.

"Yes, Your Grace," a guard said.

"I'm not going to kill you for now," Elias said. "You, my friend... will be last. I'm going to make you watch. You are going to hear their pain and feel their starvation. I'm going to make your death slow and painful."

"Your Grace, the children," Kiros said.

"Our guests are here, Taiki," King Elias said, smiling.

"Leave them out of this, they are innocent," Taiki said.

"And yet the innocent grows up and become like their fathers…violent."

"You don't know if they will become violent," Taiki replied.

"Let's not pretend, no one is ever innocent. At least not for long, my friend."

"I'm no longer your friend."

"What do you want us to do, Your Grace?" a guard asked.

"Cut off their right hands. Then, leave them here in the village, the Cursed may get hungry. Who knows, the children may get hungry and eat each other."

"Yes, Your Majesty," a guard said.

"How can you disregard the innocent and precious life of these children?" Taiki asked.

"Easily… let this be a sign of your defeat," Elias said, having the guards placing a chopping block in front of Taiki.

"Your Majesty, shall we proceed?" a guard with a sword ready to swing asked. Two other guards helped hold the child still. One grabbed its body and the other a rope attached to the hand and pulled.

"Please, I beg you don't do this." Taiki pleaded with him. "Cut me up instead!"

"Proceed," King Elias commanded.

"Yes. Your Majesty," the guard said, then swung the sword.

Screams of agony from the children caused a violent struggle as many of their parents tried to intervene but were helpless. The guards had them chained and kept beating them with whips. After this gruesome maneuver, Elias ordered the guards to return to Fog-shore, leaving the children behind in the ruins of Huron village.

Guards on horses sloshed through the soft ground as they held chains. The cold mud partially stuck to the feet of the Hurons while they were being brought back to Fog-Shore. In front of the line, guards surrounded King Elias.

"You should be happy Taiki, at least they get to go free," Elias said, as they were riding in the king's carriage.

"Free… you call this free? You left them abandoned and helpless."

"Abandoned? You brought this on your people. When you chose not to bow," Elias said. "You abandoned them."

"I see... You're distorting the truth."

"The truth is..." Elias said while placing a small

blade up to his face and leaning into Taiki. "I would have no problem with heating this knife to burn your eyes out... but I want you to see all that I'm going to accomplish and bring about. A new era has begun, and Huron village was only the beginning. I'm going to conquer this entire world," Elias said, adding pressure and nicking Taiki's face with the knife.

"Say what you will... it won't change the fact that you're still a murderer," Taiki said, not seeming to be phased by Elias cutting him.

CHAPTER
13

*E*arly the next morning, the sunlight had just began peaking over the horizon when Ollie's father, Bralden, woke up and went to the door. The wind blew as he was exiting to go to his greenhouse like usual. He went to make a new flower arrangement for Rea as he always did around that time. Out of their house and between two columns, he stepped away from the door onto the stone patio. He stopped and stood as his eyes widened and brows tightened. Taken aback, Bralden was confused to see the flowers drooping over, some of their petals lying on the ground as if someone had come and plucked them off. He stepped onto the pathway outside of his front door and looked up toward the top of the tree-line. Discolored leaves from the trees were falling, blowing in the wind for the first time. A few leaves rattled as they scraped against the stone walkway, Bralden took a step backward as they blew by his feet. He grabbed the stone frame as he returned and stood in his doorway. Bralden called for his wife to come look, but she was still comfortably covered with a blanket in the bed. He went down the hall and stood in their room's doorway, calling to his wife again, "Rea, you have to come look at this."

"Do I have to right now?" she asked. "I don't want to move right now."

"Yes Rea, you have to come take a look at this, it can't wait," Bralden said stepping to the foot of the bed and pulling on the blanket.

"Look at what?"

"Just come look," he said.

"Alright," she said, as she got out of the bed and followed him down the hallway toward the door.

"Look at outside," he said.

"What about out… side…" Rea said, losing her train of thought. She stood and witnessed the change of all the plant life. "What did you do?"

"I didn't do any of this," he replied.

"What is going on?" Rea asked, confused, while kneeling to pick up a discolored leaf from the ground.

"I don't know," Bralden said, "I was wondering the same thing."

Rea stood and watched the leaf crumble in her hand, then ran back into the house. Off the bed post, she grabbed some clothes and stuffed an arm into a sleeve. She did not bother changing her night garments as her head poked through clothing.

Bralden started following her but stopped in the doorway to look back at the trees and plants. He exhaled a sharp breath of frustration then went to where Rea was and asked, "What are you doing?"

"I'm getting dressed. I don't want to go anywhere looking like I just got out of bed," Rea replied, while she was in the middle of tightening a clothing strand around her waist.

"Where are you going?" he asked. Rea turned her head slightly.

"I don't know… I'm going to go see what is going on. I want to know are the rest of the trees and plants like this? I was thinking of going over to see Ollie and Cora," she replied.

"I just don't understand what's going on, surely I couldn't have done this," he said as he looked down the hall toward the front door, rubbing his forehead. "I have a strange feeling that I have never felt before."

"Me too," she replied coming into the hall next to him. Her hand slid across his chest as she made her way out of their home.

"I will come with you," he said, following her and

closing the door behind him.

On the stone paths through the streets, Bralden and Rea pushed opened doors, but everywhere was empty. The sound of leaves rustling in the wind continued as many that had fallen scraped against the stone walls and paths, blown in every direction. To see all the empty streets was something neither one had experienced before and gave them an uneasy feeling that something was different. On their way to the new young married couples' home, they soon discovered every place was quiet and abandoned. Homes and shop doors creaked opened and knocked against the wall as the wind whipped around them. Items that had been left out on tables were rolling off from the wind and no one was around to keep them in their places, and usually, the streets would have been full of many Tavorians by that time of day.

"Where is everyone?" Rea asked.

"I don't know, is this real or are we imagining all of this? Is this some kind of dream?" Bralden asked, as he looked around and followed closely behind Rea.

"I don't think we are dreaming," Rea said.

"Come on, let's get to their home quickly," Bralden said, picking up the pace.

Around several corners and down several pathways, they reached their son's home and knocked on Ollie's door. Bralden banged on the door first and waited, but there was no answer. Rea tried knocking, but she also received no answer, and they decided to let themselves in. Rea knocked on the opening door and announced herself as she poked her head through before entering. With a quick look around, she opened the door further and found most of their things placed nicely away, but no sign of either Ollie or Cora. She went toward the couple's room while Bralden headed to a different section of the house. The house was quiet, and the bedroom door was half opened as she gave it a knock. Its edge bumped against the wall and the door tried to close halfway on its own. The covers on the bed were bunched into a wad. Rea turned and went back to the front of the house. As she stood in the middle of the room, she looked at Bralden and said, "Neither one is there."

"They are not in the back either," Bralden replied as he stood and looked out the window.

"I'm surprised they are not here and that they would be up this early," she said and went to stand next to Bralden.

Rea looked out the window with her husband as they watched the leaves continue to fall from the branches. She saw the concerned look on his face and grabbed his hand. Their fingers interlocked with each other as she motioned for them to leave. Out the door and through the city they walked on the stone paths slowly making their way to where they knew all the Tavorians liked to feast. On top of Mount Ouranos Bralden and Rea went toward the Crown Elite. As they approached closer, they could hear a low, indistinct rumble. At the end of the walkway, they turned and saw the back of another Tavorian turning the next corner. Bralden shouted out to get his attention, but it was too late, he had gone.

"What is going on?" Bralden asked, making their way closer.

"Sounds like everyone is shouting something," Rea replied, "like they are chanting."

"Chanting?" Bralden asked.

"Yes," she replied as they stopped and listened, "but what are they chanting?"

"I can't quite make out what they are saying," Bralden replied, as they could not see anyone, but sensed they were near.

"Do you hear that?" Rea asked. "They are chanting a name."

"Who's name?" Bralden asked.

"It sounds like it is Ollie's name. You can't hear it?" Rea asked. She placed her hand behind her ear and turned toward the sound.

"Why would they be shouting our son's name?" Bralden asked.

"I have no idea," Rea said.

"Well… come on, let's hurry up," Bralden said, and went into the same corridor that they saw the other Tavorian enter.

Light was entering the covered corridor at the other end. Bralden stopped to watch as they stood in the dim tunnel. His face was half lit, but his body was hidden in the shadow. The rumble became louder as they slowly moved closer to the source. It was resonating from a large crowd. From behind them another Tavorian walked past and stepped into the light. Bralden asked him, "What is going on?"

"All the gems are ours to keep," the Tavorian replied as he stepped into the light and joined in chanting with the others.

Bralden and Rea stepped into the light behind him. Rea grabbed the man by the shoulder and turned him around. She had to shout to ask him, "Why are you shouting?"

"All the gems are ours to keep," he shouted back.

Bralden squeezed her hand and held on tightly. He leaned closer to her and shouted through what sounded like an ocean of Tavorians chanting, "Let's find Ollie. Don't let go of my hand."

"We'll find Cora too," she shouted back.

"Ollie, Ollie, Ollie…" The crowd chanted in an

almost deafening roar.

The Tavorians lifted their fists toward the sky and continued to chant as Bralden and Rea walked among them looking for Ollie and Cora. Louder and louder, voices shouted in unison as more gathered and joined the masses. It was not long before the crowd started to move. They had begun to make their way out of the gathering yards and onto the stone paths while following Bralgon. Rea grabbed her husband's arm with both hands and hung on tight so she would not lose him in the crowd. The Tavorians bumped into their shoulders almost knocking them down as they walked around the couple.

"Where are they going?" Rea asked.

"Let's wait to see where they go, then we will follow them," Bralden said. They did not move as everyone left. "We will keep our distance from them."

"Look over there, is that Ollie?" Rea asked, glancing over to her left.

"Yes, I think it is," he replied, they walked toward him.

"What is that on his head?"

"I don't know, but it looks like familiar," he answered.

"This keeps getting stranger, am I missing something?" she asked.

"It looks like he is wearing The Crown Elite on his

head," Bralden replied.

"Why does he have The Crown Elite?" Rea asked. "Look, there's Cora next to him."

"I'm going to go ask him what is going on," Bralden answered, wanting to walk closer to him.

"I'm coming with you," she said.

"Ollie, where are you going?" Bralden asked, placing his hand on his shoulder, turning him, but Ollie did not recognize his father for he was completely under the spell of the witch.

"Son, are you alright?" Rea asked, but there was no response from Ollie.

"Ollie!" Bralden stepped in front of him to stop him.

"A gift from the king," Ollie said and opened his hand.

"A what?" Bralden replied as nothing happened to him.

"All the gems are ours to keep," Ollie replied and walked past him.

"Ollie, where are you going?" Bralden asked as he followed behind, but there was no reply.

Further down the path, Ollie went with Cora at his side. This time, neither one seemed interested in holding hands as they normally would. Bralden kept trying to stop him to talk, but Ollie simply walked past his father. His eyes were only focused on the path ahead and he never would look at his father. His mind was under a strong hold and fixed on getting the new gems from other worlds.

Rea tried to talk to Cora, but they both would not respond with anything different to say. "All the gems are ours to keep," Cora replied, as she looked forward only focusing on the path.

"Stop, Son. You know I don't care about any gems," Bralden said, trying to plead with him.

Ollie continued walking as his father grabbed him by the arm again, and his mother reached for the other one to stop him. Ollie turned to the side then snatched his arm away and continued forward as they walked beside him. Cora walked on ahead as Ollie's parents slowed him down trying to speak with him. He led them to the opening of the cavern. All the Tavorians climbed down into the abyss and went to where the wall of light was located. Leading the rest of their kind, the witch stepped through to the other side with Bralgon. Bralden and Rea watched as a great number of the Tavorians entered the light's shimmering dance.

"Please, don't go. Don't leave," Ollie's parents pleaded, as Ollie moved to go between them.

Cora stepped through the wall of light. It vibrated making a low rumbling sound. Ollie followed but was several steps behind her. He reached his hand out to push through, leaving his parents behind.

CHAPTER

14

$\mathcal{F}$or several hours, traversing away from Huron village through changing terrain, Oma led Misaki and Higotji to an old abandoned path. The horses stopped at the edge of the grove and snorted. They were spooked and took several steps back. They turned in a circle wanting to run, as if they knew something dangerous was lurking nearby. Misaki leaned over, reached out her hand, and stroked her horse's neck. She spoke gently to him to calm him down. There was a presence of dark, eerie gloom over the forest, and it made both stallions want to avoid the path that was before them.

Old gray vines had entangled themselves tightly around each other. The trees looked as if they had been captured, along with anything that had ever attempted to enter the forest. Even the air felt grim as if it were caged and never allowed to leave. *It looks like almost every forest has started turning into the Forgotten Forest,* Oma thought as her horse turned in a circle. She pulled the reigns to steady and calm the horse as it pranced nervously.

"Maybe we shouldn't enter here," Misaki said, her frightened horse continuing to turn in a circle and whinny.

"Off," Oma said, patting Higotji's leg. "We will have to walk, the vines have all grown up too much," Oma said, climbing down from her horse.

"You want us to go down this path?" Misaki asked, with great concern for their safety.

"Yes," Oma replied.

"Mother, where are we going?"

"Not much further, just up ahead, we will stay in what's left of an abandoned village."

"And how do you know about this place?" Misaki asked, following behind Oma and Higotji.

"I used to live near here when I was younger."

"Hmm…" Misaki mumbled. *You lived in this place?* she thought to herself. "I thought you always lived in Huron village?"

"No, after the death of my father, my uncle and aunt took me in to care for me, but soon afterward…" Oma replied, then became silent.

"Are you going to finish telling me what happened?" Misaki asked. Her mother looked back as they made eye contact.

"After they took me in, it wasn't long before violence erupted in the village and some men killed him. It was a hard life back then. Those men took me and several other girls and repeatedly violated us. Soon, I found that I was with child and when the men learned about this, they beat me until I bled, and lost the baby."

"I'm sorry, Mother. That is horrible. Why have you never told me this before?"

"I didn't want to burden you with all of my past," Oma answered while continuing to walk.

"How did you get away from them?" Misaki asked, catching up with her mother.

"I guess when they got tired of us, I was sold to another village. There, I met your father and was freed."

"My father... what happened to him?" Misaki asked, becoming curious since Oma did not talk about him much.

"I don't know. We were separated, and he was taken away. Thankfully, it was Huron Village that found me, just before your birth. That is where you and I have remained until now. I have always dreamed of your father returning to find me one day. But I know this will never happen."

"What about your mother?"

"I never knew her… she died giving birth to me. My father always told me she was a gift from the stars and that she passed her beauty on to me. I always reminded him of her."

"So which village are we going to?" Misaki asked.

"The village of your Grandfather."

"That is the safe vil...?" Misaki began to ask.

"Get down!" Oma yelled as large birds flew out of the bushes, flying close to them, passing overhead.

"Wow, that was close," Higotji whispered.

"What kind of birds were those? I've never seen them before," Misaki asked, lifting her head up.

"Those are Elder Crows; they can become very large and are white with red beaks. They have been known to carry off small children and can kill adults when they hunt together. We call them "elder" because of the white whiskers hanging down from their beaks," Oma said, pausing for a moment. "You can still hear them… Quickly, we must continue on... this way before the large ones find us."

"You mean those weren't the large ones?" Higotji asked, following close behind.

"No… those were just younglings," Oma replied.

"Well, let's try not to disturb those things again," Misaki said, pulling on the horse's reigns.

"To answer your question from earlier, I don't

think any village is safe. It's just no one will know we are there. Let's keep moving," Oma said and made a clacking sound for her horse to follow.

.

CHAPTER
15

nce Ollie went through the wall of light and came out on the other side, the gem's mist wore off and the second part of the witch's curse took hold of each of them. He fell to his knees and then onto his hands. Ollie looked up and witnessed all his race begin to change because their bodies could not adapt to the new atmosphere they had entered. He grasped the ground and went onto his stomach. His face turned several shades of red as the veins in his neck bulged. He strained and grunted for air. He rolled over to his side as he shook on the ground from lack of the oxygen that they needed from their world. The Tavorians gasped for air. On the ground shaking violently, they all moaned and grunted in pain as their bones crackled, disfiguring them. As this painful transformation happened, most of their hair fell out into their hands as they rubbed their heads trying to fight off the torment. With mouths open and moaning, their teeth grew into sharp points. As their hands were stretched out, their fingernails became longer.

Ollie tried to crawl over to Cora, but his transformation would not allow it. He placed his head against the ground while lying on his side. He did not take his eyes off his wife. Cora turned over on her back and stared upward taking rapid, shallow breaths. She did not look like she was adjusting to where they were. Ollie, seeing that they were deceived, belly crawled over to where she was and grabbed her by the hand, trying to comfort her.

As he began to recover his bearings after his transformation, he stood and looked at his race as they continued to struggle. He tried to go back through the wall of light, but the witch had control over the wall and blocked it with a spell that would not allow any of them to escape.

Ollie reacted differently from the rest of the Tavorians. He became furious and resentful as the curse tried to take hold. He resisted and turned his anger toward the witch. Enraged, Ollie raised a hand and clinched it into a tightened fist. It was so tight that his claws dug into his palm. He made a loud growl. He set his eyes on the witch and lunged to attack it, but something grabbed his arm, slinging him to the ground. There was a loud thud as he hit the ground and debris was flung up. Lifting his head off the ground, Ollie saw that it was a massive beast with bones for horns. Bones protruded from its back forming into sharp points. Some were fractured and broken off at the tips. It had intervened and stood towering over him.

The witch glided over to Ollie and said, "If you can stand over Carcass, I will allow you to return to your home with your people."

"You never speak the truth," Ollie replied as he breathed heavily, and an unknown and unfamiliar rage came over him filling his thoughts. "When I'm done with him, I will come for you next."

Furious, Ollie stood to his feet. Ready to fight, he charged, ramming his shoulder into Carcass's stomach. They crashed into each other and fell to the ground.

With a lift from a leg flipping Ollie over off to the side, Carcass stood and uttered a massive roar. Once again standing to his feet and fighting for Cora and his people, Ollie let out a massive roar of his own. Back at it again, these aggressive brutes fought as if they were untamed animals, each determined to defeat the other. Clawing at one another, throwing punches to the face and body, they exchanged brutal blows and crashed into the terrain. Ollie dug into the ground with his hands, lifted a stone and threw it at Carcass. The huge beast was knocked off his feet and landed onto his back. With another loud growl, Carcass regained his feet and charged Ollie at full speed.

In the background, Ollie's people began to stand and make their own growls as they were hunched over. Slowly, they began making their way over to the large brutes fighting.

Out from behind the trees and stepping from the shadows, a figure came toward the witch. With a hand stretched out and bowing its head, the witch opened its hand, then turned and said, "They are rebelling, Master."

The light revealed half of his face on the right side. It was a smooth cream color. His eye had no color and was as pale as if life had left that part of his face. He stepped forward into the light and it revealed the other half of his face. Black and brown scales covered it and went down along his body and arms. His left pupil was a vertical slit like that of a pit viper. Black and surrounded with a mix of yellows and reds. Sicarius looked at the Tavorians making their approach and asked, "Whom shall I focus on?"

"That one," the witch answered and pointed its bony finger. "She is the one that he cares about most."

Cora with her breath rattling stood and focused

on the combat between Ollie and Carcass. Sicarius turned his attention toward her in order to crush their rebellion. Utilizing the strength of his power, Sicarius stretched out his hand. Into the air, Cora rose then was slammed into the ground. Her body slid across the ground coming closer to Sicarius as he began to transform her even more. Her bones made a cracking sound and broke, protruding from her flesh. He inflicted even more pain upon her as she lay helpless before him.

Just as Ollie was striking Carcass, Cora let out a scream, which caused Ollie to turn and look. With this distraction, him. Carcass blocked and took advantage by biting Ollie's arm, viciously ripping and tearing his bicep from the bone. Ollie quickly grabbed his arm as the blood gushed out. He tried to retreat taking a few steps backward but fell to the ground and onto his side. Carcass moved quickly while Ollie was down and bit him again, taking a chunk out of his back.

Ollie let out a scream of pain and bled continuously as Carcass stood over him chewing on the torn flesh. Onto his hands and knees Ollie tried to crawl towards Cora. Carcass kicked him in the ribs, sending him flying over onto his back. His breath strained even more as Carcass came and stood over him. Ollie knew he was defeated as he stared up at the ruthless beast. He looked over at Cora and reminisced about her beauty once more. Claws grabbed and lifted him up by the throat. He tried to push Carcass away with his forearm while holding his bleeding bicep.

"Forgive me, Cora," Ollie said speaking with a weak, strained voice, right before Carcass placed his mouth over his face and sucked the breath from his body. Ollie's feet twitched as his body struggled to for air. His body went limp.

A few of the Tavorians started to run and help Ollie, but Sicarius dropped them to their knees and crushed their bones. Others turned and ran away to flee after seeing their kind defeated.

Carcass dropped Ollie's body to the ground and bit him again tearing more of his flesh from the bone. Sicarius slid Ollie's lifeless body across the ground and lifted him. He hung, suspended in the air and was shown to the rest of the Tavorians, which filled them with terror. Dropping Ollie's body to the ground caused The Crown Elite to roll off his head and into the grass. It was large and sat on the ground in front of him. Sicarius placed his hand on its gold. The precious metal vibrated as scales formed and covered it all the way around and then The Crown Ellite vanished. He looked up at the Tavorians as many of them growled and snarled.

"You belong to me, now," he said, "You have a choice to go where I say, when I say, to serve me as your King. If you don't choose me… then this is what's going to happen to you."

Sicarius stretched out his hand and with one squeeze to a clinched fist, he caused Cora's ribs to crush inward, she made a moan as her breath left her chest. Her body made a jerk upward then collapsed as her ribs penetrated through her skin killing her. He quickly stretched out his hand and snatched a few more Tavorians who were standing and watching. Their crushed bodies fell to the ground.

"Now Bow," he commanded.

Many fell to their knees in fear of him, while others that did not stood motionless in fear not knowing what to do. Sicarius looked over at Carcass and said, "Now go feast."

Carcass took off after one of the Tavorians that was standing. As he closed in, the confused Tavorian took a few steps to run, but Carcass chased him down. The Tavorian fell and let out a scream as teeth penetrated the back of his neck. This sent the other Tavorians that were standing into a panic. They all began to flee trying to escape and hide as they scattered in different directions. Carcass gave chase to them after killing the one he had caught. Another one hid but the ruthless beast chased down and began feeding on him.

Now, with a horribly painful death a threat to them, the other Tavorians feared Sicarius as he enslaved their race, by allowing the witch to release the third part of the curse making them invade other worlds. Through the wall of lights, they crossed over entering new worlds farther and farther beyond their own. Sicarius sent them to help him conquer other worlds. Each time the Tavorians passed through to other worlds, they went through a different transformation. Their essences grew hostile and bodies grotesque as they committed violent deeds.

CHAPTER

16

$\mathcal{G}$**rowth** from dense vegetation covered the side of a village home. Wild vines attached themselves to the walls, trees, and anything they could touch and grew tall reaching to the rooftops. Attached to these vines, a fruit grew underneath its leaves. They were known as Fire-berries to the locals. These red fruits grew the size of two fists put together and had a sweet taste and texture like cantaloupe.

As night fell a young girl sat with her aunt inside their home sharing a large Fire-berry. While laughing together while they ate, the clear juice ran down their forearms. As they were cutting another Fire-berry in half, they were startled and became silent when the young girl's uncle named Samir barged in and said, "Take the girl and hide. The Bargolian's are here."

"Where are you going to be?" she asked.

"We have to go, Ormolu," Samir called to his wife.

"Let me grab some food to take with us," she said.

"Ormolu, no. We must go, now! They will show you no mercy if they catch either of you. We must go now… we'll get the food later, and I will be right behind you," Samir said, peaking through the cracked door.

"I got a couple of things," Ormolu said, knocking over some pots trying to rush.

Samir looked over at her and sighed with frustration. She continued to gather things before finally taking the young girl by the hand and heading toward the door.

"Alright, we need to go this way," he said.

He opened the door and made a grunt sound as he was stabbed in the stomach. Another man stabbed him in the chest, resulting in his death. Samir's wife screamed out for her husband, but it was too late. The Bargolian men had seized their home.

Several men entered the home turning over tables, ransacking the place. They had them surrounded and trapped as they grabbed Samir's wife and violently forced her down. A couple of the men dragged the kicking, screaming young teenage girl out by her hair, throwing her and locking her inside a cart-cage with other girls. Helpless and staring off into the distance, the young girl watched from within the cage pressing her face against bars, while sections of her village were set ablaze.

A slice through a thick vine-- Oma was startled by a quick swing of Misaki's blade.

"Mother, are you okay?" Misaki asked, pulling her mother out of her flashback.

"We are here, look... I was just remembering that was part of my village and... the Bargolians came and took me and several others before they torched it. I was hoping that I would never have to come back to this place," Oma said as she continued to walk.

Stepping through the thick vegetation, they arrived at the edge of the abandoned village. Dark silhouettes and shadows made the homes look full of gloom. Most of the homes were still there, but many were destroyed and those that were not had been untouched for decades.

Overgrown vines had twisted their way up the sides of the houses, while weeds had been growing for so long that many had turned into trees and were growing inside homes with caved-in roofs. The forest had stretched out, taking back what it had lost, reclaiming it once again. Most of the village homes where collapsed and rotting, with floors missing. Many were exposed to the elements, making many homes in unlivable condition. The stench of partially burned building materials could still be smelt, even after many years. Oma led them to the front of a home and stopped at the steps leading to the door of a dwelling that was mostly still intact.

"Are we going in there?" Misaki asked as she walked to stand next to her mother.

"Yes, but before we go inside, we need to make sure no one, nothing is living inside," Oma said, standing in front of the house.

"Alright, if that's what needs to be done, I will go in and make sure it is safe," Misaki said and gave the reigns of the horse to her mother.

Misaki unsheathed her sword, gripped the hilt with both hands, and cautiously approached the door. With her sword drawn, she looked back and forth slowly entering the old, dark, and musty smelling home. The floor creaked as Misaki took a step. No one had walked here in a long time, but they were not taking any chances. She looked around inside before entering. Once she passed the door it quickly slammed, making a loud popping noise, closing behind her. Startled by the sound but without any hesitation, she turned and looked, ready to strike her opponent down, but there was nothing there. A few moments later, she opened the door and stepped outside. Her blade made a high pitch sound as she placed it back into its sheath and said, "There's nothing in there."

"Good, hide the horses inside. Let's keep anything from knowing we are here," Oma said. "Do not let your guard down. I'm going to look around to see if I can find anything we can use and maybe something to eat."

"Mother, do you think it is safe to be wandering around?"

"No, that's why I said, do not let your guard down," Oma explained, giving Misaki the reigns to her horse.

"Be careful, Mother."

"Of course, I will," Oma said, walking away.

The horse snorted as Misaki handed Higotji the reigns to both her mother's horse and her own. Then she lifted a cloth on the horse's back and uncovered another sheathed sword. The hand-carved steel had an image engraved with two swords crossing and twisting together like wild vines growing.

"Now, do you know how to use this?" Misaki asked, showing him the sword.

"I have an idea of how it works," Higotji replied.

"After we get the horses inside, we will see if you really know how to use it," Misaki said, walking one of the horses inside. "If you tie the horse's reigns in a loop, all you will have to do is pull the reigns on one side and it will free them for a quick escape."

"Thank you, I will remember that," he said.

"Good, now grab your sword," she said.

He turned and lifted the cloth to retrieve the sword that she had shown him.

"Okay, I have… my sword," Higotji said, grabbing his sword from beside the horse's saddle and turning around. "Misaki? Where did you go?" he asked, but she gave no reply. Looking for her, Higotji whispered out to her again, "Misaki?"

He looked around but did not see her as everything was silent and a strange feeling of being left alone came over him. He began to walk out the door when the tip of a sword touched his temple.

"You're dead," Misaki said, "Lesson one, an enemy may not announce their attack."

"Lesson well received," he said, quickly trying to block her blade away, but Misaki countered by blocking his attack. The swords clanged together and slide blade against blade. She parried in a circle, her sword twisting his wrist taking his sword from him, sending it flying into one of the walls of the house. The sword vibrated and rocked sticking from the wall.

"Lesson two, lose your weapon… you lose your life. Now, grab your sword and try to hang on to it this time," she said.

"Understood," Higotji said, walking over to his sword, keeping his eye on Misaki, making sure that she did not try to hide again. He placed his hand across his chest, for it was still sore. "What is lesson three?"

"Lesson three, sure you're ready for it?" she asked.

"Let's have it," Higotji said as he pulled the sword from the wall.

"Even if you're wounded, the enemy will show you no mercy," Misaki said, swinging the sword at him again. Disarming him for the second time she paused, "You didn't remember lesson two," Misaki said as she went to strike him. Higotji quickly reached out his hand and his sword came flying back into his hand, just in time to block her blade.

"How did you do that?" she asked as she backed away from him.

"I don't know," Higotji answered, grabbing his chest trying to hold back the pain from his wound.

"You need to remember how to do that. Now, come with me. Unless... you want to sleep with the horses?"

CHAPTER
17

Though light from the day that would soon be fading, Oma left Misaki and Higotji to scout the surrounding village. She came to an old familiar site. It seemed like it was only yesterday that she had been there. Not sure if she wanted to enter and relive the past again, she reached her hand toward the door of her uncle's home but paused for a moment. As she came closer it was too late to turn back as her mind wandered and thought of a different time. Her wrinkled fingers stretched out against the old wood, stained with a dark green mold growing on it. With Oma slowly pushing on the door, the rusty hinges creaked as it moved open. The light shined onto the floor as most of the roof was missing and other sections had caved inward.

"Hi, Kumiko, come in... you will be staying with us, now. Are you hungry?" Ormolu asked, speaking her native tongue as Kumiko stood silent and frozen. "No? That's alright... Well... you can eat when you are ready. I'm fixing a warm pot of chick stew."

Kumiko's eyes looked down to the floor. A small white bag made of gabardine hung from one hand with a few of her things in it. Ormolu noticed that Kumiko was just remaining in place as she continued to chop an orange vegetable the shape of long pole beans. Setting the knife down, Ormolu wiped her hands against a cloth tied around her waist that she used as an apron and stepped around from the table. She came closer and lifted the young child's chin and knelt. Ormolu brushed the hair away from Kumiko's face tucking it behind her ear. Ormolu smiled and looked into Kumiko's eyes and asked, "Do you like chick stew?"

"Mmm..." the young child faintly mumbled.

"We are family, so make yourself at home. Don't be shy; if you need anything don't hesitate to ask. Oh, one more thing. I'm really sorry about your father," Ormolu said as she placed a hand on her arm. "Come, follow me. I will show you where you will be sleeping and where you can keep your things." Ormolu stood and reached out her hand for the shy Kumiko to take. "Well, come on, don't just stand there."

The young girl still did not move. Her eyes went back to the floor again as she stood motionless and her hair fell back into her face. Ormolu knelt once again and brushed Kumiko's hair from her face, then took her by the hand and said, "My dear child, I know that I cannot replace your mother or father, but you have not been left alone in this world. I shall do my best to take good care of you from now on. Come… I will show you."

Kumiko began to take a step, but there was a cracking underneath her feet. Looking down, Oma snapped back from her vision and saw that she was standing on Ormolu's bones right were the Bargolians had left her. Oma quickly stepped back to the side. She looked around, then went toward one of the back rooms. Throughout the house the floor creaked with each step. Some sections of the walls and floor were missing. Standing in the doorway, memories came flooding back of the corner she slept in so many times. There, next to the three-legged bed frame, she found an old bag that she recognized. It had turned black over the years from mildew. The material fell apart as she picked it up. A necklace and charm fell to the floor. Completely corroded, the charm fell apart, but the chain was silver and shiny as the day she had received it. A gift that was thought to have been lost, could be held and treasured again. In the center of the chain hung a small clip where the colure had been attached but was gone. Oma placed the chain around her neck for safe keeping. She tossed the old bag to the side, then carefully removed the old cloths from her bed. She took the blanket and went down the hall and into another room. Her aunts' bed had been turned over onto its side. She carefully removed its wool blanket. It smelt of rot and was covered in black mildew. She remembered getting to use her aunt's blanket a few times. *It was soft and comfortable at one time,* she thought. Once leaving the room, Oma covered what was left of her Aunt and went back to get more to cover her Uncle. Several of her own blankets were still on the bed. She used them all to cover the bones.

In the back of the house, where they all used to sleep, a tree had grown up the wall and through the roof as well as throughout the house. Oma stood looking at the tree with different shades of beautiful maroon leaves. She remembered the story Zalm had told her about the tree giants. *I wonder if this is one of them?* she thought to herself. She picked a few of the maroon colored leaves but nothing moved, not even the slightest. She waited to see if it was going to come alive and give chase to her. After a few moments, she left the room. She went back to where the bodies were and scattered the leaves carefully on top of them.

"Thank you… for taking care of me and I'm sorry

this happened to you. I hope you will rest peacefully now," Oma said. She kneeled beside where they lay and placed a few more maroon colored leaves over them. Oma left the house, closing the door behind herself.

A few houses down the same street was the house she lived in with her father. After he had passed away, no one took over and stayed in it. Their culture had taught them that it was disrespectful to live in the house of a deceased one. So, her family left it empty. When the Bargolians came, it was one of the first homes they torched in the village, thinking that it was still occupied.

CHAPTER
18

C**reak** - the old boards sounded as Misaki eased across a half-rotten porch, getting ready to enter one of the homes. She stopped and looked at Higotji. Several homes had not been torched, giving anyone many options of places to hide.

"Are you sure? You don't remember how you moved that sword?" Misaki asked, standing at the door of the next house.

"Yes, I'm sure. I have no idea. I just thought you were going to hit me, so I blocked," Higotji answered.

"Well… I was going to hit you," Misaki said.

"Really? You would have hit me?" Higotji asked.

"You would never learn to keep your weapon if I didn't. But with power like that… you're leading the way in the house," she said, waiting at the door to the next house.

"Should I knock first? See if anyone is home."

"Just open the door," she said.

"Okay. Got it," Higotji said, pushing on the door. Slowly entering through the threshold, they looked cautiously around with Misaki following behind, searching throughout the rooms.

"This one looks like we could stay here," Higotji said, lowering his sword.

"Wait… did you hear that?" Misaki asked.

"Yes… I did," Higotji replied, raising his sword.

"It sounded like it came from over here," Misaki said, walking toward the back wall.

Looking intently, she found what seemed to be a crack in the wall. Not sure what she was looking at or searching for, she found a well-disguised lever hidden, blending with the wall. With their swords drawn, Misaki snatched on the lever and a door opened with a voice inside saying…

"Wait! Don't kill us."

"You," Misaki said, with a distraught face.

"Misaki?" One of the voices asked.

"Give me one reason why I should not run my sword through your throat," Misaki said.

"Wait, you know them?" Higotji asked, placing his hand on her arm to stop her.

"Yes, I know them. Their father just destroyed our

village and killed my son," Misaki said, placing her sword up to Oaks neck.

"Wait… My father destroyed your village?" Oaks asked.

"Yes, and killed my son," Misaki said, ready to kill him.

"Please… give me a chance and I will explain. My father didn't kill Seiji. Something else did."

"You lie," Misaki said, applying more pressure with her sword.

"I swear," Oaks said, pleading for his life as the tip of Misaki's sword began to dig into his skin.

"What do you mean? Something else killed him?" Misaki asked, relieving the pressure of her sword.

"Thank you…" Oaks said, in relief.

"Well, don't get comfortable," Misaki said, keeping her sword out and pointing at him.

"Okay look… Seiji, my brother Isidore, and I found something in a cavern. We didn't know what it was, but Seiji and Isidore decided to go through. I didn't follow them when…" Oaks said, pausing in his thought as he stared ahead.

"When what?" Misaki asked.

"Umm, when I saw Seiji's head come rolling back out. And I'm sorry. I didn't know that was going to happen," Oaks said, raising his hands surrendering. "If you kill us, it's not going bring your son back. It also will not change the fact that his body and my brother, as of right now, are still on the other side," Oaks said.

"Why are you here?" Misaki asked.

"I tried to tell my father," Oaks explained. "The cavern wasn't safe when we went back to it. Inside the cavern, there was something I had never seen before. Something evil and it offered my father a crown. It caused him to kill his friend... my friend Barron. Once my father took it, the crown turned into a snake and..."

"It wrapped around his arm... That's just a dream, everyone has it," Misaki said, interrupting Oaks.

"No, it wasn't a dream this time," Tessa stammered, backing up her brother. "I wish it were only a dream. I watched it happen to my mother. That's why we are here. We left our home because there is something wrong with them."

"That would explain how your father can control the Cursed now!" Misaki said.

"He can control the Cursed?" Oaks asked.

"I'm going to be sick," Tessa said, coming out of the closet and running over to the corner of the room to puke.

"Tessa are you okay?" Oaks asked.

"We are never going to be able to go home now," Tessa said, leaning over with her head against the wall.

"Have you seen anyone else here in this village?" Higotji asked.

"We haven't been here that long. We heard something and quickly decided to hide," Tessa said.

"We need to make sure no one else is here and we must find my mother. Come, you can stay with us," Misaki said, turning and allowing Oaks to walk out of the room.

"Are you going to kill them?" Higotji asked, pulling Misaki aside whispering to her after Oaks and Tessa left the room, continuing outside the house.

"No, they are more useful alive... for now," Misaki said.

"Surely, you won't make them pay for the mistakes of their father."

"I can't make any promises."

"They had nothing to do with what their father chose to do."

"Their father murdered and destroyed my village. So... like I said, I can't make any promises. Now, get out of my way, we need to go find my mother," Misaki said, leaving Higotji in the house. She joined Oaks and Tessa, giving them a treacherous smile on her way outside to lead the way, looking for her mother.

"When did my father attack your village?" Tessa asked, cautiously approaching Misaki.

"Earlier... around mid-day. He showed up with his

men," Misaki replied, while they were walking.

"We had no idea he was going to do that. I know it may not mean much, but I am very sorry for what my father did," Tessa said.

"Wait here," Misaki said, stopping and turned halfway around as she kept her hand on the hilt of her sword. She saw her mother standing off in the distance facing the forest tree line. "I'll be right back."

Standing between two rotten trees with her head tilted down and rocking back and forth slightly, Oma was mumbling softly to herself. It sounded as if she was grunting. Misaki approached her cautiously for she had never heard her making this sound before. Concerned for her mother, Misaki placed her hand on Oma's shoulder and gently asked, "Mother, are you okay? What are you doing?"

"This is where my father is buried and... I was speaking with him about you and things that have happened," she replied.

"You were speaking? I never heard you say any-thing, you were grunting," Misaki said.

"That is how I speak where I'm from," Oma replied.

"You never taught me to speak that way," she said.

"That's because it's a dead language, and no one who speaks it is living."

"Mother, you are the last of your kind."

"No, you are my kind, you just don't speak a dead

language," Oma replied. "I wish he could have met you."

"I wish I could have met him too. Here, would you like to place a flower on his grave?" Misaki asked as she walked over picking a white winter plum blossom near where she stood.

"Thank you," Oma said, she knelt and placed the wilting plum blossom on her father's graveside. Standing, Oma turned to Misaki and gave her a hug and asked, "Where is Higotji?"

"Mother, we have a problem. Higotji and I found Oaks and Tessa hiding in one of the houses."

"What? How do they know about this place?" Oma asked.

"I don't know, but they claim there is something wrong with their father and mother."

"Something wrong with their father... yeah, he is a murderer."

"There's more... Oaks told us he was there when Seiji was killed, and his father didn't do it... that something else killed him."

"Do you think he is lying, covering for his father, or just trying to save his own life?"

"I'm not sure what to believe, Mother."

"I want to speak with them," Oma said.

"Mother... There is something else. Do you remember when you used to tell me, whatever you do... don't let the snake in?"

"Yes, I would tell you that before you fell asleep."

"They both are saying they witnessed the dream that everyone has, actually happen."

"He told me this would happen."

"Who?"

"Cree told me," Oma said.

"Your friend, The Oouek told you?"

"Yes," she replied.

"I thought Cree was someone you made up for a story?"

"No, he was very real. He's the one who told me whatever you do, don't let the snake in. Cree said that there would be one who would rise, one who would hunger for power, and that he would make way for the Ruthless One."

"A ruthless one? Are you saying somebody is leading the way for the Ruthless One right now?"

"Yes."

"You mean Elias?" Misaki asked. "He wanted us to bow to him... You mean there is someone coming that is worse than him?"

"I can't say for sure if it is Elias. I don't know who that person will be, and Cree never gave their name," Oma said.

"I will go back and run my sword through him."

"Misaki, please... I know you are angry, but I beg of you not to go back there. And please, don't sneak off while I'm asleep… Promise."

"Okay, I won't sneak off."

"Promise me," Oma insisted

"I swear, Mother. I won't sneak off."

"It is getting late we need to find shelter while we still can see," Oma said.

"We found a place where we all can stay for tonight," Misaki said as she and Oma walked to where she had left Oaks and Tessa.

Higotji was sitting on a porch near a rotten wall in between some of the abandon homes. Next to him, Oaks and Tessa where talking when Misaki and her Mother arrived. He noticed them walking toward their direction and spoke, "We were just talking about where to stay."

"It's this way," Misaki said, and went in the direction where she and Higotji found Oaks and Tessa.

CHAPTER
19

Numberless years and countless decades had passed since the Tavorians were conquered and dispersed. They were slaves without shackles of iron chains. Forced into going through different worlds, they went and were never allowed to return to their own. Those who would not do as they were commanded tried to escape. Many ran, trying to hide themselves, but they only failed at the attempt as they were hunted down.

The time of watching the sun fade and having long celebrations and a long rest through the night became nothing more than an old memory. A memory that for some was buried deep inside like the gems in the ground back home. Those that survived believed everything they knew and loved had become lost.

To the best of their knowledge, their way of life was stolen, gone forever.

Trapped between worlds, stars rotated in their owns systems as others crossed into neighboring star systems. Some stuck out from the ground and rose to rotate in the skies. There were many suns and moons with light connecting them all. These suns only glowed and did not burn anything that they encountered. The suns had suns and the moons had moons. Countless they were as they moved in all directions, but nighttime never came no matter how far the suns moved in the endless ages of their existence. Sleep was not an option even though their bodies felt the weight of a prolonged wakefulness. Even if they could sleep, the risk was too great for them to close their eyes in the ever-changing misty glades they called the Timeless Immersion.

Frightened and running to escape the clutches of certain death if caught, Bralgon tired and slowed until his motion was a jog. Then, he was only able to walk dragging his feet. Finally, exhausted, he stopped to catch his breath. He turned and stared into the distance, but nothing was there as he flopped down onto the trees. They did not break but only made stress sounds as they bent. He wiped the sweat from his forehead with the back of his hand and grunted. His dark eyes looked to the ground as he desired to stretch out and rest. *When will this be over? I will just go ahead and give up. I no longer care anymore about living like this. I hope he finds me so I can be done with all the hiding. I'm running no further.* He told himself. The whites of his eyes were bloodshot, and his eyelids were heavy as he sat and made up in his mind that he was not going to move again. He reached down and slid a rough, brown pouch covered with dirt stains into his lap. His pointy fingers flipped the bronze latch open. He kept it locked and secured over his shoulder. The only time he considered taking it off was to toss stones when he was back home. He flipped open the top and removed it from around his thick, dirty neck. Bralgon carried it everywhere because it was the only thing he owned that he had received from his mother.

Bralgon sat in discomfort while resting on the treetops. His breath rattled as he inhaled and exhaled. With his weight bending the tree trunks, he almost squashed them. As he sat, they folded over, looking like nothing more than weak blades of grass. He had been running and hiding ever since the death of Ollie and Cora and many others of his kind. To keep his life, he tried everything to remain hidden and far away. The great hunt was the game Carcass liked to play, and it was now Bralgon's turn to endure the ruthless encounter. Even when he was not around, the dread of him was as strong as if he were always watching. As

Bralgon sat, something felt different. The invincible, always present and fear seemed to be there, but it had two things it did not have before: a name and a face. The long obscurity was a faceless and starved creature that seemed to creep and loom about. Its name was unknown for so long, but as it soon gained a name, it was now all clear to Bralgon. This stealer was death, and Carcass did its bidding. *Maybe death won't hurt that bad...maybe he will make it happen quickly, so I won't feel it,* he thought. He remained sitting, nervously waiting for Carcass to come. Maybe his attack would come from somewhere along the tree line.

To rest once again, he reflected on his friends and the long-awaited chance to be home. The laughter from the once filled cavern flooded his mind as he reached into the pouch. The flap leaned against his leg as he turned over his clinched fist and opened his palm slowly, staring at the jewel. His face reflected on its surface. He made another grunt and furrowed his eyebrows as he did not like what was shown. The shimmer kept his attention occupied. He continued to stare at the only thing he had that was worth anything from his world, Argon: the cherished Dahlia gem that Ollie and Cora gave to him. It sparkled in the reflective light.

As something small moved in the corner of his eye, Bralgon turned his face, looked up, and away from his gem. *Good, death has finally arrived,* he thought. His eyes squinted as he was expecting to find Carcass ready to start ripping into his flesh as payment for his disobedience to Sicarius. It was something smaller, almost unnoticeable. Bralgon leaned forward and made eye contact with Seiji. The Tavorian's eyes widened as his breath quickened and heart began to race. He clinched the Dahlia gem tight in his hand. It was as if an urge came over his body to go after the small creature.

Being spotted, Seiji stood frozen like a statue, afraid and too nervous to move even an inch yet still fascinated by the giant on the trees. The thought of running crossed his mind, but he only wanted to stare just a few moments longer.

Out of nowhere, a hand wrapped around his body and lifted him. Toward the skies and stars, he went rapidly. It happened so fast; he did not have time to scream. A quick snap of teeth, biting his head off, Carcass spit to the side, sending Seiji's head bouncing and rolling through the wall of light that he had just come through. Carcass took the small creature's body and turned it upside-down. Blood and water came forth from Seiji's neck as the monster drank his blood.

Carcass took a moment to look at The Tavorian. They stared at each other as Bralgon sat and waited for his turn to die. Carcass growled, as he opened his mouth wide. His breath was warm and looked like a wave of heat. He gave one final look at Bralgon, then turned to walked away. The ground rumbled as he was not as careful with his footsteps and went off into the distance. He carried Seiji's body with him and disappeared over the horizon.

CHAPTER
20

The guard in The overgrown gardens that belonged to the Queen. The greenery had blocked everything except the stone path in front of him. He turned and followed its narrow walkway leading to the stone arches. No one was around as he carefully watched out for those who belonged to the King and Queen now. There, under the curved stones, another set of doors led to the outside. Along the stone wall and down the steps, he looked straight ahead, trying to remain calm as he walked past other guards standing at their posts. They stood and stared straight ahead. Around the corner and in the distance were the docks and the Great Echo Room eased the door closed as he made his exit quietly. He walked into the ships. The urge to look over his shoulder to see if he was being followed was strong, so he went into another alley and around a corner. Once past the turn, he quickly placed his back against the wall. He kept his hand on the hilt of his sword ready to unsheathe it at any moment as he peeked back around the corner. His dark eyes stared, fixed toward the alleyway's end. Every finger in his glove gripped the hilt tightly as he took deep breaths to calm himself. With his other hand, he unsheathed a small dagger and raised it next to his face ready to strike with the point.

Several of the people from Fog-shore walked past the alley, but none came into its entrance. *Alright move,* he told himself as he continued to stare down the walkway. Away from the wall, he took off down the alleyway and then into another at the end just in case he was being followed. Along this walkway, there were more locals and trading venues. He bumped shoulders with them as he calmly went toward the docks. If he were being followed it would now be difficult for a pursuer to catch him, but it would also be harder for him to tell who was after him unless they started pushing others out of the way.

Just up ahead through the crowd, the crossing at the docks came in view. There at the end near the railings, two guards stood at their post protecting its entry. A voice close to him called out for him to stop, but he kept walking ignoring the command. Pulling back a sleeve, he showed a mark that looked as if it was branded into his flesh, and the guards kindly stepped aside to let him pass. Before crossing over the walk bridge to the ship, he spoke to them saying, "If anyone tries to cross and they don't have the mark, don't let them come aboard."

"Aye, Sir," the guard replied and stepped back into place.

When the crew member was halfway across the gangplank, a guard from Fog-shore was stopped by the other two as he tried to go between them. "Sir, I command you to stop." But he attempted to cross anyway and ignored the guard's command.

The guards from the crew grabbed the Fog-shore guard by the arms to keep him from getting on board. Only one of them did the talking as they both made the guard from Fog-shore step back. "Sir, I can't let you pass if you don't have the crew's mark."

"By the decree of King Elias, I order you to step aside, before you and your entire crew lose your lives. The King wants to see all who sail these waterways including you and everyone aboard this vessel. I will only tell you one more time to step aside. This ship has been seized by the order of King Elias," the guard said as he gripped his sword and unsheathed it halfway.

"Sir, would you allow me to take you to our Quartermaster?" the crew member asked.

"Lead the way," he replied, and followed.

They walked across the gangplank leading to the ship's steps that took them down onto the main deck. Many of the men were working to keep the ship clean and make any repairs that may have been needed after time out to sea. The old boards from the ship creaked as one of the high-ranking crew members walked toward them. The crew's guard pointed and said, "He's the one you want to talk with."

"Mmm," the Fog-shore man replied and nodded his head as the guard turned to go back to his post.

The ship creaked as it rocked slightly while moored to the dock. Waves lapped softly at the side of the boat. In the gentle wind, birds soared and continued to squawk. The guard from Fog-shore made his way down the last few steps and looked around the ship until his eyes locked with the one in charge.

"How may I help you?" the high-ranking crew member asked.

"By the decree of King Elias, I order you and your crew to forfeit this vessel and accompany me to stand before His Grace," the guard replied.

"And if we refuse?"

"You will…" the guard replied but stopped talking abruptly.

His chest lifted upward as a knife pierced his lower back. A hand reached around and grabbed him by the throat. The knife was twisted back and forth several times, as a voice spoke into his ear, "I know you thought that I didn't see you following me, but you were wrong. Your king just killed my brother Mason and ruined all the plans we had for this place. I want you to know something. In this life or the next, never trust a Bargolian."

He pulled the knife out and slung him to the ground. The armor crashed against the deck as he fell facing the sky. A knee came quickly and pinned against his chest. The crew's guard jabbed the blade rapidly in between the cracks of his helm several times. The king's guard's body twitched a few times and his armor clanged before he went limp. When the crewman stood over the lifeless man, blood dripped from the blade as he breathed heavily. With a quick flick of his wrist, he slung the blood off but kept the small dagger at his side.

"Prepare the ship to leave, now," the guard said, standing over the body.

"Where is Mason?" the one that had been pointed out as the Quartermaster asked.

"Give the signal for all to come aboard and get us underway," the guard replied.

"I want to know where Mason is?" he asked.

"He's dead," the guard replied. He pulled off his helm and slung it onto the deck. The metal rang as he unsheathed his sword and lifted it along with his dagger, pointing them at the man. Many of the other men stood watching as some stopped what they were doing to listen. "I will slice all of your throats and watch your pathetic lives fade from your bodies if you ask one more question. Now get us underway and out of this port before we all join him."

"My apologies, Sir Drift, I didn't recognize you," the guard replied. "What about the other men?"

"That is why I said give the signal. If they are not here when the timer is up, they will all be left behind, and trust me you don't want that. We are going to be outnumbered very soon," he replied lowering his blades.

"Make readyyy!" the Quartermaster shouted.

The men scrambled to their positions, lifting anchors, tightening rigging, and checking the sails. In the crow's nest of the main mast a crew member with a metal mallet pounded the ship's bell. The first hit from the man was to warm the metal to keep it from cracking, followed by a second and third. It was the fourth hit that was loudest, it started the signal which was a pattern that was repeated several times. The locals that heard the signal, paid no attention to its ringing, for the ships rang their bells regularly while entering and leaving the port of Fog-shore. Those who heard the ship's bell ringing and knew to do so always found a way to look toward the ship to see what colors were flying.

Aboard Mason's ship the color of each banner raised had its own meaning and only the crew members of that ship knew what they were for. There were five colors that were raised on the ship's three masts. The black banners meant that there was a death aboard the ship and usually only flew if the ship was out to sea. When a fellow member fell ill and died, they often would be buried at sea. Their body would be sewn into a shroud that was weighted so that it would sink. Then it would silently be slid into the waves. When the red banners were raised it was a signal for an attack of killing and plunder, whether it be at sea against another ship or onto some other land. White banners were for scouting new lands such as islands or continents while remaining peaceful and tactical. The green banners meant that the ship was leaving portside and there was little time to get aboard. If there was no banner flying it meant the ship was staying in port. The last color had never been used the entire time that Mason led the crew. Its color meant to drop everything that you were doing, abandon all, and to return to the ship for your life depended on it.

Another guard rang a smaller bell below to signal 'All hands, on deck.' The crew rushed topside to find that blue flags were flying following the ringing of the ships bell. Many of the crew stopped to watch as the wind caught the banners. They ruffled, stretching out completely while being raised on the Mizzenmast and the Foremast. Men climbed quickly up into the shrouds with their lookout glasses. The spotters watched toward the land for other incoming crew members and to see if Fog-shore's guards were gearing up to attack.

The lookout in the crow's nest had a small glass filled with sand that he poured over a fine net collecting the sand into another glass. Once the sand filled the second glass, he poured it back into the first glass. This time, once the sand was gone, he rang the bell for a second warning. As he poured the sand, he watched and waited to ring the bell for a third and final time.

CHAPTER
21

*C*alm and silent, the forest remained as evening time came. The light shining through the trees was fading fast. Closing the door behind them, Oaks, Tessa, Higotji, Misaki, and Oma all went into the house where Oaks and Tessa had been found hiding. They brought every item they found inside and prepared to settle down for the night. Oaks placed his bag against the middle of the back wall for a pillow and rolled out a small blanket to cover up with when he went to sleep. Tessa knelt and watched Misaki as she did not want to take her eyes off her. Oaks noticed the soon-to-be awkward look that she was making and tried to distract her.

"Here," Oaks said. Looking over at his sister, he handed her a blanket. "You can roll it out next to mine if want."

"Okay," Tessa said, moving to spread the thick quilt out. She leaned over and whispered to her brother, "Don't leave me alone with them."

"I won't," he whispered back.

"Are we going to sneak away later?" she asked.

"I don't know, it seems Misaki is watching every move we make," he replied.

"Just another reason why I don't trust her," Tessa replied. The door closed with a clunking thud. They both looked to the door. "It's going to be hard to get away now."

To make sure that the entrance was secure, Oma placed a piece of wood in front of the door, bracing it for extra precaution. Misaki placed another piece of wood that she found against the hinged side, then turned and faced her mother.

"Alright, that should give us a little warning before anyone, or anything, tries to get in," Misaki said, pulling on the door. "What do you think?"

"May not hold for long, but I think it will be good enough... at least for tonight," Oma replied.

"Good, well I'm going to talk to them," Misaki said, starting to walk.

"Wait," Oma said, she gently took hold of her daughter's arm and spoke in their native tongue. "I think it may be better if I talk with them."

"Yes, I think it may be for the best if you do that," she replied with a sharp tone but speaking where only Oma could understand.

"Misaki, they are not their father, and they did not do what he did, or choose their parents," Oma replied as she slid her hand down Misaki's arm and held her hand.

"I just want him to pay for what he has done and let him see how it feels to lose someone you love," she replied. Her eyes almost wanted to form tears as her forehead tightened.

"That is not our way," Oma said with a look of concern in her eyes.

"Perhaps we should consider changing our ways, Mother," Misaki replied. "Kill as they kill."

"Please don't say that, don't forget about the compassion that I taught you to have. Because if you don't, then you will be no different than their father."

"He killed our people and you speak of compassion, … friendliness? Is that what you want? All of us to be friends now? Live like nothing ever happened?" Misaki objected.

"Misaki," Oma said stopping her. "We all have lost loved ones. They have; we have. Both sides have lost and killing them will solve nothing. Come, let us rest tonight and clear our thoughts."

"If that's what you want," she replied.

"It's not about what I want, but what is best for now," Oma said as she brushed a strand of hair away from Misaki's face. "Just think for a moment, and not respond only with your anger."

"How? All I see when I close my eyes is my son's bloody face."

"And if you kill them, then you will see their faces also... Come, I will help you fix a place to sleep," Oma replied and led her toward the wall where there were old blankets pushed in a pile against the corner.

The gray floor planks creaked as Oma and Misaki knelt to spread out the blankets. Dust had covered them, but the cloth remained in somewhat good condition since it had not been exposed to the changing elements of the weather. Misaki laid down on her side and stared at the golden pattern of floral designs on the wall. Leaning over her, Oma spoke softly saying, "Get some rest, I will check on everyone else."

"Yes," Misaki replied with a sniffling sound.

"I love you," Oma said, then gave her a kiss on the cheek as she had done many times before.

Oma softly grunted as she held onto the wall to ease herself off the floor. *I'm too old for getting up and down from the floor,* she thought as she leaned forward with a hunched back. Her muscles and joints ached as she walked toward Higotji. He was sitting with his back against the wall and leaning his head back. Alone, he sat, opening his eyes when he heard the floor creak and Oma's feet scuffed against the planks. She stood next to him and asked, "How is your wound? Do you want me to take a look?"

"I'm okay; it's still a little tender," he answered, pulling back his clothing and showing his wound.

"Here's a blanket for you. We should be able to rest here for a few days," Oma replied as she knelt and pulled his bandage back to see. His skin was almost pale but still red around the gash that was closed and slowly healing. "I will try to find some leaves and make you some of my tea in the morning."

"You don't have to do that. I know it's too dangerous out there," Higotji replied with a raspy breath.

"We can't stay in here forever. We're going to have to eat and drink eventually, and if it's my time to die, I will go doing what I love to do," she replied.

"And what is it you love doing?" inquired Higotji.

"Helping others," she replied.

"Oma, you are too generous. Thank you for everything you are doing for me!" Higotji said.

"Don't worry, Higotji, you don't have to thank me. Just get some rest. I'm going to go check on Oaks and his sister," Oma said, getting up and leaving him.

Across the room, Oaks and Tessa were in the corner that was near Higotji arranging the few things they had brought with them. Getting ready to settle for the night, they constantly kept glancing over at Misaki and her mother.

"Do you think they are going to do anything to us?" Tessa asked, whispering quietly to her brother.

"I don't know," he replied. "If Misaki were going to kill us, she had the chance when her sword was up to my neck."

"Well... I don't trust them," Tessa said, putting her head down, turning away and pretending like nothing was going on. Oma came and sat next to them. "Hi... Oma, how are you?" Tessa asked, with a fraudulent smile.

"So, where were the two of you going?" Oma asked.

"We are going to our aunt's village," Oaks replied, looking over at Tessa, for he did most of the talking.

"And, where would that be?" Oma asked.

"Our Mother's sister lives in Sathorn."

"Sathorn?" Oma asked. "That's quite far from here."

"Have you ever been there?" Oaks asked.

"No... I've seen it from a distance," Oma replied, and paused in thought for a moment. *I remember looking through the bars as a slave girl, wanting to escape from the cage cart and flee to the massive kingdom. But I was never allowed to go near the city,* she wanted to say. "I... I also, have always wanted to go there."

"We've never been there, either," Oaks said.

"Do you know how to get there?" Oma asked.

"Not exactly," Oaks replied.

"How are you going to find Sathorn, if you never been?" Oma asked.

"Our Mother told us about her sister, and that she lives in Sathorn."

"Have you ever met your aunt?"

"No." Oaks replied as Tessa looked down fidgeting with the corner string of her blanket.

"How do you even know she still lives there?"

"We know her name. I'm sure we will find her," Oaks stated confidently.

"It's a dangerous path from here to there. I could show you the way if you would like," Oma offered.

"I will talk to my sister and get back to you."

"Sure… rest here for the night and we will talk again in the morning," Oma said as she stood and looked at Oaks' sister. "Oh, Tessa… to answer your question of how I'm doing, I'm just concerned about what is to come for all of us."

"Me too," Tessa responded. "We have no place to go, and I just want to go home and have everything return to normal again. I miss my home and sitting in front of my mirror brushing my hair."

"None of us have a place to go to now. Maybe one

day, you can call somewhere home again. Get some rest," Oma replied, she turned, and her feet scuffed against the floor once more. She went over next to Misaki and eased to the floor. Then she stretched out and covered herself with the blanket.

The dusk light coming in through the cracks soon faded as twilight faded and the uneasiness of darkness crept in bringing a cold night. Sharp howls and sudden whirls sounded as the frigid air whistled throughout the night. Roofs vibrated, and leaves that never fell scraped against the outside walls. The gusty wind brought northern air which kept them from falling asleep for quite some time. After hours of staring into blackness, their eyelids became heavy and drowsiness took over. Held captive by the night, one cannot help but fall victim to the desire for sleep.

Several hours had passed and everyone was fast asleep. With a deep breath, Tessa exhaled and turned over onto her side to get comfortable in her sleep. Her necklace slipped out of her shirt softly touching the floor. The trinket opened into two different parts, casting a soft blue glow onto Higotji and partly onto Oma while they slept. Stepping away from the shadows a dark figure knelt halfway into the light beside Oma, touched her on the arm, and gently shook her calling out her name.

"Wake up… Oma, wake up," the soft whisper spoke.

"What is it?" Oma asked, mumbling and exhausted. Her eyelids were heavy as she blinked trying to gain focus.

"It's me wake up," the soft voice whispered once again.

"I'm awake," Oma whispered, then yawned quite loudly.

"Ssh," he hushed her again. *"Not too loud, don't wake everyone…"*

"Is that really you?" Oma asked, he was glowing a brilliant blue.

"Yes, it's been a longs time since I've seen you… Ah, just look at you… and you're still shining over the heavens," the voice whispered, holding her hand.

"I'm wrinkled and old now and…" Oma said, but the voice interrupted her.

"And still as beautiful as ever."

"Where… how did you get here?"

"From the blood of innocents, life is born."

"What do you mean? And how is that possible?" Oma asked.

"Things are changing," the voice said.

"Changing?" Oma asked, confused.

"Yes, you need to get ready."

"Ready for what? I'm too feeble now," she replied.

"This," the voice said, reaching out and opening his

palms.

"What is it?" she asked.

"Look, and see," he replied. Oma squinted; she was slow to look away from his eyes.

"Am I dreaming?" she asked.

"No, you are awake," he replied and extended his hands. *"Just look and see."*

"What is it that I will see?" she asked. She watched as he raised his eyebrows and said nothing but seemed to answer with only his eyes.

His hands glowed a light blue that was bright and sparkled as she looked down toward them. He quickly moved forward and covered her eyes with his hands. A bright light of rich indigo color flashed and seemed to twirl against her eyes. It was a dance of shadows pulsing from blue to black. A sickness was spreading, spilling over, grabbing hold of everything it could touch. There Oma stood in the midst of chaos, when a voice behind her bellowed out, then echoed from below her as she was lifted up and turned. The voice shouted, "Protect the Maiden!!!"

More and more voices shouted, some with familiar faces. They all screamed the same thing beckoning every form of life, even the trees, to come alive and fight. Their roots remained deep in the ground until it was too late. The sickness was upon everything in the forest. Swift and merciless it moved. It was like a raging river that flowed, carving a new canyon through the ground. It came quickly destroying everything it touched. A form like thick dark blood twisted and rose from the liquid. The creature turned and showed its face. It opened its mouth to hiss and was ready to strike with its poison fangs. Its eyes had slits for pupils, and it looked as if it could see Oma. On each hand his fingers turned into two more sets of fangs that were ready to attack. All around was a great battle that raged. Up from the ground the tree roots struck the creature, but its poison began to turn them a deep maroon color. The Maiden turned to Oma, placed her hand over her chest and said, "You are the new Maiden now." Then she sacrificed herself to contain the poison inside the forest. Two sharp fangs struck and released their poison into her flesh.

"Ah!" Oma let out a scream, jolting awake, she sat up quickly.

"Mother-" Misaki shouted waking up, she turned over to check on her mother, "Are you okay? You... you look different."

"I feel like..."

"Like you're younger?!" Misaki asked, in shock. "Because... you look beautiful and about fifty years younger."

"What?" Oma raised her voice, pushing up her

sleeves looking at her arms. "This is impossible. My wrinkles… gone, do you see any wrinkles on my face?"

"No, what is going on Mother?"

l

"I… don't know. I thought I was dreaming," Oma replied.

"The snake dream again?"

"Sort of, but this time... there was no snake body and scales, but I could see its face... I believe it was real."

"What happened?" Misaki asked.

"Nothing... I don't want to discuss it right now," Oma said, looking over and realizing that Tessa was now staring at her.

"Where is Higotji?" Oma asked.

"He's outside with my brother," Tessa replied.

"How long have you been awake?" Oma asked when the door quickly swung open.

"What's going on?" Oaks asked, as he and Higotji rushed through the door with swords drawn.

"Nothing," Misaki said.

"We heard a scream," Oaks said, walking over next to Tessa.

"Oma? You're..." Higotji said.

"Beautiful," Oaks blurted out, staring at her in awe.

"She's way too old for you," Tessa said, rolling her eyes while she lifted her brother's jaw, closing his mouth.

"Thanks," Oaks said, with a sarcastic tone and half a smile, moving her hand away from his face.

"You said you weren't going to leave me alone with them," Tessa said, whispering to him as they began to talk privately.

"I'm not, I thought you might would like a little time for yourself this morning," Oaks said, whispering back to her.

"Oma, how are you looking so young now?" Higotji asked, extending his hand, offering to help her stand.

"I don't know... when I awoke things seemed to appear normal, but Misaki noticed that I looked different."

"Different? Mother, I have never seen anyone as beautiful as you."

"That's strange... about as strange as what I wanted to speak with you about," said Higotji. "I heard Oaks going outside this morning. So, I got up to go out with him and that's when I noticed my pain its almost gone. Look... my wound has healed a lot more this morning. It's not fully healed, but it's a lot better. How can that happen so quickly?"

"If I knew... I would share it with you," Oma said, pausing. "A dream… did you have a dream last night?"

"No, but I see what your father was talking about," Higotji replied.

"My father?" Oma asked.

"Yes, when he said your mother's beauty was a gift from the stars, and she passed it on to you. I believe him," Higotji said, smiling.

"Oma," Oaks said, speaking up.

"Yes," Oma replied.

"I talked with my sister and we would like it if you would show us the way to Sathorn, please," Oaks said.

"I can show you the way, but the journey will be long and a hard one," Oma replied.

"Shall we get going?" Oaks asked.

"We will... but not today. We will need to gather as much food, water, and whatever else we may need before we can start the journey," she replied.

"Mother, you want us to go to Sathorn?" Misaki asked, in a quick, harsh tone.

"Yes, I think we should go," Oma suggested.

"Why there?" Misaki asked.

"Because... we have nowhere else to live," Oma explained. "Look around we can't stay here, there's nothing here. It could be a new start. All of us."

"You may be right... *but I don't want to live with them,*" Misaki said changing her language so only her mother would understand.

"This place is big, and you won't have to ever see them again once we are all there," Oma replied in their own tongue.

"Is everything alright?" Oaks asked, interrupting

them.

"Yes," Oma replied and smiled. "She was saying that she didn't like it here and that she was going to find food for us to take with us."

"Good, because I don't want to stay here any longer than I have too," Tessa spoke up.

"I will go and gather what food I can find for us," Misaki said, as she made a fake smile.

"Higotji will you..." Oma began to speak.

"Yes, I will go help her," Higotji said, interrupting Oma.

"Mother, are you sure you will be alright by yourself here with just them?" Misaki asked, while speaking their language.

"I'm sure I will be fine," she replied and struck the air with a few of the martial arts techniques that she remembered. Her movements were with ease and as graceful as she had done when she was younger.

"What was that about?" Oaks asked.

"I'm just remembering my techniques," she answered.

"Well you have fast moves," Oaks said.

"I'm just warming up," Oma said as she stopped and knelt to fold her blanket. She looked up at Misaki. "I will stay here and look for some more things that we can use."

"I will be back soon, Mother," Misaki replied.

"Oh, and Misaki, be careful and remember, it's not safe for any of us anywhere around here," Oma said, turning to pick up her bag, then emptying it.

"Yes Mother," she said and went out the door with Higotji.

"What do you want us to do?" Oaks asked, watching them leave.

"I will need both yours and your sister's help here," Oma said.

"And what sort of help is that?" Tessa asked, she crossed her hands against her stomach and raised her eyebrows.

"I believe nothing knows we are here, but if it learns we are here, this place will need to be able to keep us safe for at least one more night," she replied. "So, I need both of you to follow me."

"Sure, lead the way," Oaks replied and followed.

CHAPTER
22

"I **don't** understand. Why are we giving the retreat signal? We have never retreated from anyone, Sir," the Quartermaster said, as he followed behind Drift.

Into Mason's cabin, the younger brother Drift went, shedding his amour. Once in the room, he stopped and looked around for a moment. He was taller and stronger than Mason, but his way with words of persuasion did not come close to his brother's. He was the one who was appointed to secretly carry out many of the killings for Mason.

"We will no longer be staying in Fog-shore," Drift replied as he opened the doors to a cupboard. Inside there were hanging skins of thick fur. All of them were dark brown and black except two. One was white and the other was a rare ash color. "Everything we've been working toward is now lost, and anyone that remains here is at risk."

"Everything? What about the coin and everything we have been working toward?" he asked.

"Even the coin," Drift replied. "The hope for what all the coin was going to achieve here will soon not mean anything."

"How is that possible?" the Quartermaster asked, looking toward the small windowpanes. The bells rang for a second time.

"Do you hear that?" he asked, as he slid his arms into the sleeves of one of the dark furs. "Once they ring for a third time, we are gone. If you saw what I have seen, the crew members onshore are lucky we are waiting around for any of them. So, you are welcome. Anyone left here, will soon meet their end."

"Where do we set the course to, Sir?" he asked.

"We head north. My brothers need to know what has happened. In a few days, we will return to our home and more than likely my brothers will decide that if our people will be at war with the people of Fog-shore."

"Sir, it may take longer than a few days to reach Nor-Fall. The seas will be starting to freeze," the Quartermaster replied.

"Which name do you prefer?" Drift asked.

"I'm sorry, Sir... name?" he asked.

"Yes, which name do you prefer to be called? Everyone on board calls you the Quartermaster. Is that what you prefer?"

"My name is Peek, Sir. But you may call me which ever you prefer," he replied.

"And how long has it been that you have been away from home, Peek?" He asked.

"I couldn't say for sure, Sir," Peek replied.

"Do you remember the northern Narwal?"

"Of course, who can forget the stories about them, Sir? They can break a ship apart with ease," he answered.

"They also break apart the ice as they make their northern migration..."

"Those creatures are said to only be but rumors among crew members and children, Sir," Peek said, interrupting Drift.

"No, not rumors," he replied.

"How can you be so sure?"

"Because, I have seen the creatures with my own eyes, and the routes they take," Drift replied, as he pulled a rolled-up parchment from Mason's cabinet.

"What is this? Peek asked as Drift unfolded the yellow material.

"These charts are old, and no one has seen them outside of my family. They show the routes that we shall take as the rumored Narwhal's break through the ice and provide passage for us."

"Forgive me, Sir, if what you're saying is true, they could kill us all. The crew may not want to go willingly, especially if it's going to lead them to their death by sea creatures," he replied.

"So, don't tell them,"

"Yes, they could kill us, that's why we are going to keep our distance. We're going to follow them and let them do the work for us.

Study the maps. They don't leave this room. Then set the course and get us underway," Drift said.

The rapid pounding of several knocks rattled the thin door. Peek rolled up the parchment as Drift turned the latch. In the doorway stood another crew member who was breathing heavily because of running from the docks. He was a skinny, young crew member with a pointy face and bushy brown hair that looked like it had never been brushed. The young boy could not have been any older than fourteen. He was a runner whose job was only to report back his findings to the Quartermaster. Drift looked at the boy and asked, "Yes… what is it you want?"

"They're not letting anyone out of Fog-shore," the boy replied.

"Mouse, what do you mean they're not letting anyone out?" the Quartermaster asked.

"Sorry, Sir," the boy replied, he blinked rapidly and rubbed his head. "What I meant to say was the guards are not letting anyone leave Fog-shore. They are closing gates."

"Are you certain of this, boy?" the Quartermaster asked.

"Yes, I'm sure of it, Sir." Mouse replied nodding his head.

"Have them sound the alarm again; we have to leave now," Drift commanded.

"Sir, it's too soon. The other crew members may need that extra time to get aboard," Peek said.

"Time is up! Study the map. It doesn't leave this room… Understand?" Drift asked, tightening his forehead as he looked at the Quartermaster.

"Yes, Sir," he replied as he opened the map.

Drift turned and walked out closing the door behind himself. The sun shined on the dark fur as he stepped out from shadow of the hall onto the main deck. Mouse had followed him out and stood next to him. He put an eyeglass to the boy's chest, and said, "Here, climb up quickly and see if you see any of our crew running toward the ship."

"Yes, Sir," Mouse replied.

Up the brown rope of squares tied with knots, he climbed. Mouse moved quickly as other crew members raced across the gangplank to board. Mouse scrambled nearly to the top of the rigging, wrapped an arm through the one of the squares, and extended the glass. Through the streets of the markets, he focused to see if anyone was running their way. Drift looked up at the boy and shouted, "How many do you see?"

"There, Sir," Mouse replied pointing. "I count at least five, and they are running."

"How far away are they?"

"They will never make it if we leave now, Sir," Mouse replied.

"How much sand is remaining?" Drift asked.

Mouse climbed higher until he reached the wooden mast. He grabbed on to its wooden handles for climbing. To the crow's nest, he climbed and reached to its edge. There, another crew member was watching the sand collect in the glass. Mouse looked at the two glasses, and asked, "How much longer before the bells ring again?"

"It won't be long now," the man replied.

"Drift is ready to leave now," Mouse said. He looked through the glass one more time to see how much closer the other crew members were getting. He reached out, took hold of a rope, and slid down to the main deck where Drift was waiting.

"What did you find?" Drift asked.

"There's more crew members on their way and the sand is almost into the next jar," Mouse answered.

"So, they won't make it even if we wait?" Drift asked.

"No, they are too far away," he replied.

"Then, time is up," Drift said. He walked over to another bell and rang it loudly.

Crew members continued to cross over the bridge planks in a rush to board the ship. The last two guards crossed as the large bell sounded its' final call. The planks made a thud as the guards slid them onto the deck. Other crewmen came and helped the guards, they worked together to place the boards against the ships rail. Then they cast off the lines that had secured the ship to the dock.

The water splashed against the hull as the ship creaked and pulled away from the docks to cut through the waters. Drift stood with his looking glass watching out ahead as another crew member followed his instructions at the wooden wheel and guided them toward the open oceans. The ropes tightened and the sails expanded as they filled with wind. The crew quickly took to their positions ready to serve. Mouse was near Drift as they passed where other boats were docked and said, "Sir, there are smaller boats blocking the way."

"I see them," Drift replied as he continued to look through the spyglass.

"Slow us down," the crewman at the helm shouted

out.

"No," Drift shouted. "Full speed ahead!"

"Sir, we will crash into them," the crew member replied.

"Ram whatever is in our way. We are not stopping for anyone," Drift commanded. "Ring the bell again."

"Aye, Sir," the crew member replied.

The ship picked up speed while the large bell above rang out a warning to those ahead sitting still in the water. Small boats that could be operated by one person quickly paddled out of the way as the large ship showed no sign of slowing as it sailed on the water highway. Some of the bigger vessels could not move quickly enough as Mason's ship made its approach. The crew member at the helm shouted, "Brace for impact!"

The ship's bow and beak went between the two smaller ships as the sides of the hull scraped against them pushing them out of the way. Mason's ship held together as it crashed into a third blocking the way. The beak pushed the other ship over onto its side. Water rushed into the bottom as wood broke. It was not long before it started to sink. The other ship's crew members jumped into the water trying to flee as the large ship plowed over everything in its path.

Guards from Fog-shore ran toward the harbor gates in a race to make sure that they were closed and to give support to the others that were already there at their posts. More guards climbed into their boats to go after Mason's ship. The two ships that they scraped against rocked and spun. Once the crew members from the other ships had straightened, they also joined in the game of chase. Off in the distance, Drift continued to watch through the eyeglass as they came closer to the gates. The gates were not closed all the way, but ropes held them together. Other ships began to close in on them as Drift tried to pick up speed.

Drift closed his eyeglass and tucked it away behind his back. Several of his crew members gathered around the helm, but when they saw the closed gates they backed away from the rails.

"Sir, the gates are closed," Mouse said.

"We are leaving Fog-shore now," Drift replied to the group of men as they neared the closed gates. "Go through the middle of the gates. We're going to smash it and break through their ropes."

The route where the larger ships traveled was closed and was not going to open for them even though they showed no sign of slowing. Strong ropes wrapped around iron bars held the gates closed. The wood and iron were thick enough to have a walk space on top of them. They shifted back and forth slightly, creating a small opening as the ocean current continually changed. Small waves hit against the corrosion of rust and salt that had built up over the years near the bottom of the gates. The guards from Fog-shore abandoned their post on top of the gate as Mason's ship rammed into it. Wood from the gate cracked and splintered as ropes tightened around the iron. The bow protruded most of the way from the opening but was stopped as the mass pressed against the ropes.

Drift and his men braced themselves as the ship came to a halt. Some were thrown to floor of the main deck. Water sprayed upward behind splashing the stern. Mouse's feet flung forward as he hung on to the ship's shroud and came crashing back down. The ship rocked and shook and was pushed back from the gates. Two ships came up from behind blocking them in. Grappling hooks where tossed over to the rails to secure them.

Drift looked over at the crew member at the wooden wheel and said, "You are the new Quartermaster."

"But, Sir, …" he began.

"Do whatever you must for yourself and the rest of the crew," Drift interrupted, as he left the main deck headed for his cabin.

"Aye, Sir," the wheelsman replied. Another grappling hook hit the deck, slid across the planks, and attached to the railing of Mason's ship.

CHAPTER
23

Countless still shafts of golden sunlight beamed through the myriad leaves of the forest, illuminating small patches of verdant serenity. The ancient dynasty of Mirentis soaked up as much sun as possible, focusing its energy through thick glass and runes toward a central seedling nested on a pedestal shaped wooden trunk that was cocooned with green string like vines. In the depths of the forest, away from the trampling of other creatures, this seedling bloomed once a century throughout recorded Oouek history having been given to them by a queen of old. A blossom of aetheric energy beamed outward from the pod, briefly lighting the area in a bright, brilliant blue. Deep inside at the core was the power to create life which was known by all as the Young

Maiden of Theriac. With a cracking sound, the grand flower opened. Its petals that looked like smooth silk unfolded, almost as if a rose, heeding the call of mother nature herself. Each petal brought forth the resplendence of nature in its own color, shining in every color of the rainbow and more, from a single flower. Those who bore witness to the event were said to be either the luckiest of the Ooueks, or the darkest of powers, poised to possess the bloom. For several thousand years, this centennial bathed with blood those who would possess the heart of nature itself.

The wide flower finally appeared in its full glory. At the pinnacle of the sun's arc, a blue beam shot outward, returning a gift to the giver. From the aether, a Demi-Arch Fey emerged, infantile in the first moments. Yawning and stretching her flexible limbs to explore the new world in which she awoke. Her torso resembled that of a nubile young woman, her features the allure of almost any creature. From her resting spot on the rainbow rose, she floated into the air to explore. Her limbs unfolded from each other. Through the branches, she stretched from the very nature of her being, plant like, with twisting vines and tree limbs.

It all seemed familiar, as if she had been here countless times. Her mind raced to find a semblance of memory, a core to latch onto, or even something that would give her the faintest idea of where she was. Her head jolted as a memory suddenly bored into her. A sword pierced her heart and bright red eyes stared devilishly into her soul. She remembered dying and her aetheric being seeping back into the lifeblood of the world she once knew. Her powerful magic was captured to be used against the worlds and its creation that she was supposed to protect. She embodied nature.

The Young Maiden looked at a stone hedge as her limbs slid across its rough surface and haunted screams sounded in the distance. Soon the cries became louder and approached closer. Yells and shouts grew coming from different directions. Metal clanged upon metal. The forest seemed to speak to her, giving her visions of groups running away and others staying to fight. Some came to harm her, others to protect. She floated in midair, her skin turning blue as she concentrated. All around her the forest came to life. Trees reached down to snatch those that would do her harm. As she bent nature to her will, memories started flowing. Once more in relative safety, she examined them and could see that she was now surrounded by creatures of all types.

"Protect the Maiden!" a voice bellowed from below her in the temple as hundreds of people rushed in carrying spears and swords. The shadows moved closer to the Young Maiden. They knelt before her offering their services and loyalty. They used their power to bring forth gold from the ground. Into the air, gold pillars twisted and locked together. Being surrounded by a cage of spun gold and protected by barriers, she could only begin to comprehend why she was kept encapsulated. She put her hand out to offer aid, but a barrier only blocked her as her skin flickered with a blue glow. She quickly realized that while being protected, she was also at the mercy of those protecting her.

A plume of fire erupted from the door, blasting many away and incinerating those immediately in the front lines. Creatures baring their teeth and claws started to pour in through the windows and doors, as they were bent on taking the prize of the century. She did not know where to look as they were coming through at every angle. She screamed inside her domed prison, fruitlessly while trying to shake loose the golden bars, to flee. It did not take her long to realize that her protectors faced overwhelming odds and that her life was all but forfeit. A huge door collapsed with a bang as more monsters poured into the temple. They were gigantic and smashed everything in their paths.

She snapped back from her vision as the shadows stood with her. They surrounded and faced away from her as they stared into the forest. One of the shadow creatures turned to her and asked, "Are you alright, Your Majesty?"

"The giant creatures are here," she replied as her eyes widened with a look of concern that quickly came over her face.

"I am sorry, but that would be the Tavorians, Your Majesty," he answered.

"What is your name?" she asked.

"My name is Cree, Your Majesty. I am a shadow master," he replied. "But don't worry, I have a plan."

Her eyes rolled upward as she was taken to another vision. An inky blackness crept in from beyond. She realized that she did not know what lay beyond those doors before her, but she knew something of the forest and where it stretched. The shields only weakened her, preventing her retreat, or aiding those who fought and now died for her. The blackness took the form of a humanoid. It grabbed at anything close to it, even its own kind at times, draining them of their essence and tossing them aside.

Terror rose in her throat as she realized it was there for her. Her prison would be her tomb if she stayed. Desperately, she pounded against the golden barrier as she struck at it with all the force she could muster. She entangled her hand in a huge clump of roots and swung it with all her might. The resounding force vibrated and echoed around her like a gong, but the barrier did not break. She realized all too late, that her powers had been weakened by being cut off from the forest. Again, she struck, as a hammer against steel, but the golden bars would not budge.

She watched the scene unfolding below her as the Ooueks were fighting and dying. The black creature had taken to killing them individually, now that they knew there was no hope. Each drained corpse was discarded carelessly. She screamed and thrashed trying to free herself. Then she screamed more, to protect those who were dying. As she looked down to see the Arch Oouek staring up at her, she heard him scream as a tendril pierced his flesh. The blue aether waivered.

"I... I'm... sorry..." the elder said as he coughed.

Blood spouted from his eyes as inky hooks tore him apart. The shield disappeared entirely. The Dryad realized she was alone in the temple, surrounded by a horde of beasts with the sole intent of killing her. She grabbed the smoothed bars and screamed as something snapped. Angered, she lashed out from the golden cage with her own tendrils, sending roots into the ground from high above. Immediately, the creature latched onto one of her attackers. Her anger would not relent, despite the pain of wanting to save and protect her defenders.

The temple trembled, shuddering slowly at first.

Massive roots suddenly burst through walls, vines as thick as a man's leg snaked through the throng and started to crush her attackers. Some of the Tavorians grabbed her limbs to control her. She could feel her life force being drained by the dark creature below her. She flexed her roots, commanding nature to help her. The temple seemed to twist. Elaborate stone pillars jostled ever so slightly as dust floated off the ancient stone. Grating noise stopped everything in the room except her and the evil trying to kill her.

Another scream tore itself from her throat as the stones gave way. Pillars collapsed to the ground and broke. Cracks opened all over the ground, swallowing some of the smaller creatures and crushing others in their wakes. The temple itself started to crumble with massive rocks crushing entire wings of the sacred space. A brief glimpse of the twilight sun streaked across her face and made her glow a soft blue as the outside world flooded into the building. It quickly faded into a memory as the ceiling came toppling down upon the inky black creature and her as the world went still.

Tears streamed down her face. In a memory from centuries ago, the ruins all around her reflected the destruction she had just witnessed. Confusion whispered in the terror that rose within her. The memories that flooded in gave her only piecemeal flashbacks of the story, a story that twisted, with massive holes. She looked at the Shadow Master but was taken back into her vision once again. She felt the dark creature again. Once more, he was coming for her with an insatiable hunger. Instantly, anger rose within her and she resolved to prevail against the monster, now that she was free. She plunged her root-like limbs into the ground and saw he was racing toward her.

She brought a tree bough down, knocking the unsuspecting creature away with every bit of force she could muster. The beast disappeared into the brush, temporarily dissipating to an unknown darkness. With her senses of the forest all around her, she could still feel a creature approaching her. When she wheeled to face it, the smiling face of an older Oouek found hers. With her anger still aroused, she struggled not to take immediate action and regarded the being with caution.

"You… don't remember me… do you?" he said with surety. She understood him without needing to try, and slowly shook her head, no. "I am sorry that your birth always seems to come with such mayhem and confusion. You are the Lady of the Mirentis Forest, one of the royal seeds of the highest Queen. You are here to protect the forest, to give life, and to keep the balance of nature. We are here to protect you."

She noticed that within her focus hundreds of creatures had emerged from the forest surrounding the ruins. With great variety of race, creed, culture, and sex, they came. Each carried a pendant that she recognized as the rose bed that had brought her to this realm. Without words, the Oouek placed a leaf in her hand holding a large bead of liquid. She drank it without question, recalling this exact memory. In an instant, all the memories flooded into her mind.

A younger version of the Oouek sat in front of her. It was the Shadow Master. The darkness was defeated for the time being. The rose had already begun to wilt, yet she remained. They walked from the ruins, heading deeper into the forest toward a tree. It was the Queen's tree. Its massive branches towered above anything in the landscape, casting its own shadow on the forest. She listened intently to the Shadow Master as they walked, enjoying the conversation, and learning about the changes in their world.

"These massive trees bear the seeds of many like you and of course many of their own kin and maintain the serene balance between life and death. You are the guardian of this one," the Shadow Master droned in his honey-like voice.

The path was still easy because she floated a few inches above the ground. The tree seemed to be a daunting life force, ancient and full of mystery.

"I don't know what to do," she replied.

"We will help guide you, as we have done many times before. It seems that you are born every hundred years in a cycle we do not fully understand. However, you have been here when dire times arise."

"What of the darkness then? What is this thing that hunts me?" she asked, eager to learn more and remember the past.

"We are not sure of that either. The Queen has not told us, yet, but she has commanded us to protect you. Many beings in this realm are attuned to magic sources. They want to harness the powers that you possess for themselves," the Shadow Master whispered as if quiet would ease the burden of knowledge. "Every time you are reincarnated, it stirs a great evil in the land, and it seems to find you. Sometimes we win, and you can see many years of life… other times… we are not so fortunate. I am sorry, My Lady."

"You have done your best. You have nothing for which to apologize. It seems that even if I die, I always return. Yet, if your kind give their lives for mine… then they do not return," she replied with a certain formality. "I… hate that you must suffer that loss because of me."

A glittering tear fell from her cheeks, followed by more. As each landed, a small flower sprouted, leaving a tiny glade of wildflowers. The Oouek patted her shoulder trying to console her. After several minutes of the weight settling on her shoulders, she realized this was only one time in the many cycles. How many more would she have? How many more would suffer because of her? Desperate thoughts crowded her mind, threatening to overwhelm her emotions.

"We know the price, My Lady. Each of us took the oath to protect you and the forest. We know the dangers out there, and together we can put an end to them. Please do not be sad. Now come, we have more to discuss."

As she wiped her face with her palm, her vision cleared, and many more memories washed over her. She now could recognize many friends from her previous lives. She wanted to start friendly conversations to get caught up on stories and the lives of those she once knew. She felt happy amongst them, even though something started to creep into her mind. The stories did not seem to add up properly. It had not been a century since she remembered some of these tales.

"Elder Shadow Master why am I here?" she asked suddenly to the Oouek. The crowd around her went silent.

"My Lady, it is your centennial birth. You come every hundred years, since the Queen left," Cree replied, even though she could tell something was wrong.

"These memories and stories do not add up." She pointed to a young Oouek. "I remember her face. She was little more than a child when I saw her last."

"Errrr... Yes... My Lady... that would have been... forty years ago." His answer caught in his throat. A dark shiver ran up her spine. She turned to face a charging beast and lost consciousness as the world sank from her mind again.

A maniacal laughter filled the air all around the glade. The Ooueks fought desperately against overwhelming odds as she awoke. Unlike other times, her consciousness returned intact. The fresh death of her body nearly twenty years ago was just a faint memory of cold steel splitting her. She instantly realized that they were in danger as the world threatened to become unbalanced. She set to the task of clearing the glade, commanding the trees, using the earth, and even striking down enemies with her bare hands. An endless torrent came and went.

She fought her way through any creatures not carrying the seed pendant, ripping them apart as she tried to rally her friends and protectors. The stench of blood filled her nostrils, her glade tinted red with the carnage. Even though she had cleared the glade, she did not catch the one she knew would be there, the creature of darkness. She expanded her roots, seeking through the forest to pinpoint it. Everywhere she looked, Ooueks fought innumerable foes that were trying to consume the land. Unfortunately, each place lacked the being she sought.

"Where is it?" she demanded of her allies as she looked at them.

Nobody could answer, each face had already been hard pressed in the battle. Commanding the woods, she quickly turned the tide of battle into their favor in many areas. Her mastery over the land had not had a chance to diminish yet, and her powers came easily. Her skin started to glow an iridescent blue as she floated into the sky. Her vision expanded in all directions, yet nothing of the shadow she knew was there.

Suddenly, it felt as if a spine forced its way through her soul. She looked downward, fully anticipating a sword to be jutting from her chest. Blue blood glittered from an opening that was not drawn by a mortal weapon. Another strike ripped through her body from an unseen foe. She screamed in agony as a third blow seemed to sever something vital as she fell. Ooueks rushed to catch her body, but the impact flattened them to the ground. She struggled to stand, her chest on fire, the droplets of blood staining the forest.

"What is happening?" Many of the Ooueks cried,

looking around to find the assailant. The glade was silent, every enemy eradicated. She cried out again with the pain threatening to overwhelm her senses. They tried to heal her, but the unknown wounds proved difficult. Suddenly, the reality of the situation hit her.

"THE TREE, PROTECT THE TREE!!!" She screeched. Her words echoed through the woods. The forest came to life with her command. Trees uprooted to protect and fight alongside the Ooueks. Even the animals obeying the call rushed out of hiding to attack. It became a mad dash to get to the tree. She tried to float, but her powers were weakened, as if the life blood of the forest had been drained from her.

As they crested the final ridge to the sacred grove, she staggered. The towering tree was wilted, bereft of almost all foliage. At the base, the dark creature wrapped its inky tendrils into the life system of the trunk. She screamed again as another lance coursed through her, piercing the trunk. She knew the tree was dying and rushed to save it. Before she could take another hundred paces, the weight of the world brought her to her knees. The forest stopped and looked to her.

The battle cries died out, and the animals went rushing back into the woods as the trees paused. A jarring crack thumped through the air sending pollen falling off the surrounding trees. Echoing thuds raced up the tree as the internal structure splintered. Every set of eyes stared in abject horror as the base of the mother tree caved under the creature's attack. The sides of the support column blew out with an ear-splitting sound. Once one column fell, the rest of the tree twisted on its base, ripping the structure apart. Then, as if in slow motion, the monumental tree fell to the forces of gravity.

Tears streamed down her face as the dark figure sent its poison into the trees, turning them a maroon color. The trees reached out, grabbed hold of the Ooueks, and pulled them into the old trunks transforming them into part of the trees.

When she could finally compose herself, she looked up to where the mighty tree had once proudly stood. Given the loss of the Ooueks, she thought the world would never recover from such an atrocity. Her fully restored memories counted back through time to the dawn of the forest. She had failed in her responsibilities to protect the tree and the delicate balance of nature. The massive trunk still rested on the forest floor, a token reminder of the finality of death.

"Why... How?" she asked as the words almost caught in her throat. "How is it that the tree is dead, yet I live? Am I not tied to the tree?"

"My dear Lady… I know this is a shock, but you should know as all things, that nature is a cycle. A new sapling lives, yet it is fragile and weak. It exists within the trunk of the Queen's tree. We have hidden it to keep it secret, for this one is not the Queen's tree, but only a distraction," Cree replied as The Maiden snapped back from her vision.

"That would explain why my powers have waned," she sighed. "I have failed you all. I will not allow this to happen again."

"You have not failed; you have stayed the course for thousands of years. It has all been for the Queen. We will not abandon you now," Cree replied.

The nods of the Shadow Master surrounding her warmed her heart. The faces of family and friends gave her the strength and courage to rise. Just as the sprout grew towards the sky, she would see that it flourished once again, and balance restored. She looked at Cree one more time as her blood fell to the ground. She cupped her hand as it filled with her blue blood. She placed it to his mouth for him drink, and said, "From the blood of the innocent, comes life. Now you will never die."

CHAPTER

24

"Send in another one," Queen Sienna ordered.

"Yes, Your Majesty," Kiros replied giving a half bow as he turned and went to the doors of The Great Echo Hall.

Queen Sienna stood in the middle of the steps leading up to her throne. Her dark eyes looked around the room as bodies from their home of Fog-shore to lay passed out. The motionless bodies were all women. The gold from her crown shined and the white diamonds sparkled in the light. Even the dark gems flickered at the right angle and reflected against her dark hair. Many sections of the roof of the hall were made of glass that cast a soft blue tone onto the floor.

The bulky iron doors closed as Kiros went out, he

was not gone but a moment when they creaked opened again, the latch making a clank as he reentered. Queen Sienna did not have enough time to make it to the top of the stairs before Kiros brought two more people in. They stopped just inside of the doorway wanting to go no further. The Mammoth grabbed a fist-full of their clothing in each hand and twisted. He pushed them along gripping tightly as they walked toward the Queen.

"Forward," he commanded with a harsh tone.

The middle-aged couple did not know why they had been summoned. *We have not done anything to deserve any punishment,* the husband thought. The mother squeezed the hand of her daughter and pulled her along as they walked.

"I'm scared Mommy," the child said as they went in, stepping between the unconscious bodies of people that had entered before them.

"Sssh! Child," the mother replied. Her daughter came closer to her leg. Only half of her cheek was showing as she tried to hide. She wanted to look away but hung onto to her mother tightly.

"It's alright to fear little one," the Queen replied. She met them at the bottom of the stairs with her arms at her side. She was watching the little girl as she covered herself with her mother's clothing. "As you should fear."

"Where is Elias?" the husband spoke up. His brow tightened because he did not like Kiros having hold of his clothes.

Kiros gave him another nudge before letting go of them. He stood on the main floor close behind them to keep the couple in place. The Mammoth watched them closely in case either of them tried to escape and reminded them to be humble before the Queen.

"Do you think that knowing where he may be will change anything?" Queen Sienna asked as she continued to look at the child.

"Yes," he replied, with a crude tone. "What have you done with him? And what are you doing to everyone?"

"Do you speak on the behalf of your family, or do you speak for yourself?" the Queen asked cutting her eyes over at him.

The man's lip lifted as he thought but was not sure how to answer. The Mammoth gave a shove to the man's back. He almost lost his balance as he adjusted his clothing and straightened his back looking over his shoulder. The Mammoth with his deep and harsh voice said, "You answer when the Queen asks you something."

"They know how to speak," he replied as he locked eyes with the Queen.

"I want to see and speak with Elias," demanded the

man.

"King Elias is waiting for you," she replied and knelt to put her attention back on the daughter.

"I don't see him," he replied.

"You will," she said, as she reached out her hand toward the child. "Would you like to touch my crown?"

"What does that mean? You will?" he asked.

The Queen did not answer as the little girl revealed more of her face. Her little face was round with blushed cheeks. When she smiled her front teeth were missing and the tips of her new ones had just started to show. Soon the young girl stepped out from behind her mother and stood before the Queen, but her father was becoming frustrated. He exhaled quickly as the Queen asked the child again, "Do you want to touch my crown?"

"I asked you a question," her father said interrupting the Queen. "And I want to know what you mean? What are we doing here?"

"First things first," she replied as the child reached her hand toward the crown.

"Don't touch…" the father started to say, but the Mammoth grabbed him, reached around, and covered the man's mouth.

The man mumbled as his wife turned her head to look at him. He struggled as the Mammoth held him with both arms. Her eyes widened when she turned back to her daughter, but it was too late. The young child had already reached out and touched the sparkle of the crown. Its gold stuck to her finger as her mother pulled her away. She brought her hand back and looked at her fingers. Around the tip and down her tiny fingers, it moved like a spilled liquid as it started to spread. It covered her entire hand and rotated around her arm, moving upward. The child let out a high pitch scream and flung her hand to shake off the gold. Diamond shaped scales formed in the reflective liquid and would not let go of her flesh. The pitch of her voice became higher as it carried several times throughout The Great Echo Hall.

From the stone floor, several bodies stood, rushed over, and grabbed the mother, holding her still. She tried to pull away from them, but there were too many of them that held her tightly. Veins bulged from her neck as her face turned several shades of red. Her lip curled and her yellow teeth bared, she was filled with anger when she screamed at the queen, "What did you do to my child?!"

The ones that were holding the mother stretched out her arm with the palm facing up. Queen Sienna walked over to her as she tried to pull her hand away, but the others held it outstretched. Queen Sienna stood in front of her as the woman's child stopped screaming. The mother looked at the child as the little one stood facing the throne. Queen Sienna grabbed the mothers face, turned it toward herself, and leaned in. With a soft tone, she spoke, "You want to know what I have done?"

"Yes," the woman replied nodding her head.

"It will be better if I show you. Then you will know why you are here," the Queen replied. The woman gasped as their eyes locked. She held back her instinct to scream. Queen Sienna poked her flesh dragging the finger trinket she was wearing along the mother's forearm. The trinket broke the skin as the Queen scratched all the way down to her skinny wrist and into her palm.

"Why are you trying to kill us?" The woman asked as she looked at the blood from her forearm.

"On the contrary, you will serve a greater purpose," she replied.

"I don't want to serve anything… what did you do to me?" The woman asked as her eyes rolled back and her knees went weak. The others held her up right.

"You can't fight it," the Queen replied. "You will soon sleep for a little while and when you awake after seeing the master, you will have your instructions."

"My daughter… please… don't… hurt… her," she implored, her eyes becoming heavier. She saw her daughter's face one last time before it blurred, and the mother closed her eyes. She heard the Queen's voice when the young child turned toward the Queen.

"Go play in the grass little snake," the Queen said. The little girl turned and skipped to the door. A guard opened the door for her to leave.

CHAPTER
25

Overwhelmed by a growing sickness, the forest looked spent, and showed little signs of life, or ever growing anything that had rich bright colors again. Most of the trees appeared weak to the touch with gray vines that had grown upward twisted around their trunks. The limbs that were not broken drooped almost touching the ground and had never discarded their maroon leaves. The ground was covered with moss and ferns that had once grown in luscious green colors but were now discolored darkened by the stain of rot.

"This doesn't look anything like I had imagined," Misaki said as she stood in front of the maroon woods.

"You've never been here?" Higotji asked.

"No, this is the forest my mother use to describe

to me when I was younger," Misaki said as she had placed a hand on one of the trunks. "I wish they were all still alive."

"I'm sure they were all beautiful once," Higotji replied reaching out to touch a hanging limb.

"We will have to go further out from this forest if we are to find something to eat."

"Do you know where you are going?" he asked as she squatted to get a better view of the direction they needed to go.

"Don't worry, my mother taught me how to track," she replied and gave a nod and stood. "This way."

Under the limbs she stepped leading them through the forests. The leaves on a branch rattled as Higotji let go and followed Misaki. They walked a great distance before they stopped at the edge of an opening in the trees, and grasses of all kinds grew. The sun shined on the fields and offered a little warmth. The winter grasses that grew in the fields produced the fruits of the wild bush. Higotji stepped around Misaki out into the grass. His hand rubbed against the green growth that was waist high. He inquired, "Can you see it?"

"See what?" she asked.

"It's a sign of hope," he replied turning to face her. He closed his eyes and lifted his face to the sky. His arms were outstretched as grass danced against his hands, and the sun beat on his face.

"What do you mean?" she asked.

"It's a place where the decay and rot has not touched," he replied with a smile taking a deep breath.

"I don't want to live here. I want to go back home. I want my son and husband back," she replied walking out from under the trees into the fields.

Higotji followed as Misaki led them through the wild bush. The fields had not produced their harvest yet. To the next tree line, she took them to where the pine woods grew, and the teak-raven trees shed their bark. She could identify them by their rich brown color and the shavings they left on the ground. Through the crunching and popping of bark, Misaki and Higotji scavenged searching throughout the forest for any kind of food they could take with them on their journey to Sathorn. Higotji followed Misaki for Oma had taught her which types of plants could be collected and used for medicine and which ones could be eaten.

"This is something we can take with us. We call these Wild Mallow and the leaves are quite tasty. Here, try one," Misaki said softly, picking some leaves and handing them to Higotji.

"Mm..." Higotji said. Closing his eyes, he gave a half smile while savoring the taste.

"Eat up; this plant can grow almost anywhere, the whole plant is edible, all the way down to the roots," she said snapping the stem in two.

"Yeah… these do taste good," Higotji replied. He picked and placed some into his bag. He also ate a few more.

"Look," she said as she hurried over to a large bush and picked some fruit tossing one to him. "These are fire-berries… try it. My Mother loves to eat them."

"Wow, I can see why she likes them, these are quite delicious," he replied, taking another bite. The sweet juices popped out, while the fruit dissolved quickly in his mouth. He pulled more of them from the stem.

"I take it you like them?" she asked.

"Yeah, we need to have more of these," he said, picking more of the berries and stuffing them into his bag.

Looking across the way, he saw more of the fire-berries and went to gather them. A strange creature caught his attention as it came buzzing past his head. He ducked out of the way and followed but kept his distance. The creature landed on a branch not far from him and turned its head. It brushed around its head with its front legs for a moment to clean itself. Higotji moved slowly toward it.

"What are you doing?" Misaki asked, seeing him sneak toward the creature and stare.

"Have you ever seen one of those before?" Higotji asked. As he moved closer, the creature flew to another branch. Moving the branch out of the way, he inched closer.

"No… I wouldn't mess with it," Misaki replied, and continued to fill her bag.

"I just want to have a closer look," Higotji said, kneeling to watch this strange looking insect.

The bark snapped as he tried to ease closer and closer toward it. He hoped it would not fly away before he could get a better look at it. The creature flexed its wings with a flutter as if it were ready to take flight once again. Its body looked black but had many colors on it that reflected in the light. Its wings were transparent but also reflected color at a certain angle. The creature turned and spit a small, clear, sparkling stone at him then vanished quickly.

"Did you see that?" Higotji asked, but Misaki did not reply for she was busy filling her bag.

To get a better view, Higotji picked up the stone and held it up and in the light. There was something bright the size of a small seed flexing and rotating inside. He squinted as he watched it move and flicker. *That is strange, maybe I shouldn't touch it,* he thought to himself.

Misaki continued gathering and stuffing as much food into her bag as it could hold. She closed her bag and latched the strap. As she turned to look at Higotji, they were both startled by a loud, eerie sound. They could hear agitated screeching and thrashing not too far away. She ran hunched over to where Higotji was kneeling and placed a hand on his arm.

"Let's go, I think we need to get out of here," Misaki said, while she squatted down quickly next to him to avoid being seen by whatever was making terrifying sounds.

"What was that?" he asked. He lifted his head to see.

"I have no idea... it could be an elder crow, we might want to leave," Misaki said, but Higotji took off and went through the trees with her trailing behind. "You're going the wrong way, what are you doing?"

Higotji, ran through the forest ducking under limbs and jumping over logs, then stopped. Misaki caught up and stood next to him. He looked at her while catching his breath and said, "I want to see what it is."

"Some things are better left alone. Especially in these parts of the woods," she said.

"Look, I'm sorry, but I must go and at least see what it is," he said and went toward the repeating shriek.

"He's going to get us killed," she whispered to herself and followed down a cliff after him. "I can't believe I'm doing this."

He ran across a small field and into the dead forest. Not sure what direction to go, he stood still and listened for the sound again. His eyes scoured the terrain for any movement. The noise sounded once again. Higotji headed toward the high pitch shrieks, running faster not to lose it again. At the edge of the tree-line, he hid behind some trunks hoping to see the source of the sounds. Misaki came up next to him and peaked out around the other side.

"Do you see anything?" he asked softly

"No," she replied.

Higotji eased across the open space toward the boulders that blocked his view. Misaki shook her head and exhaled with frustration. She turned and looked behind to see if they were followed. She took a few more deep breaths, then moved up beside Higotji. The loud wailing continued, but they still could not see what was making all the commotion. Looking around the gray stones and down below, they saw it near the other side of the gorge. They both ducked back down to avoid being seen. A deed of cruel punishment being carried out, and a helpless creature was there to receive its wrath.

Dust rose from the ground as the creature flailed its wings while thrashing its tail in a desperate attempt to get away. Hunched behind the boulders on the edge of a small ledge, Higotji and Misaki remained unseen while they kept their distance. The Cursed had captured a small dragon and were keeping it from flying away. They held it down with their bodies as a dark material entrapped its wings and feet and wove around its neck. The material spread attaching to the dragon's snout, wrapping around it and squeezing. The creature struggled fiercely for its life, blowing small breaths of fire from its nearly closed mouth. Every movement seemed to ensnare the dragon more as if it were entangled in a web. Surrounded by the Cursed, there was nowhere for the dragon to go.

Misaki looked across the way to the tree line above the gorge as The Cursed emerged from the forest and charged aggressively toward the creature. Down into the gorge they dropped wasting no time in joining in the attack. Some appeared from the gorge's stone wall that the dragon was near. Swarmed, the creature was unable to escape as they tried their best to kill it. The Cursed continued to scratch and bite viciously to inflict excruciating pain.

Having compassion for the creature, Higotji decided to go and stop the attack.

"Where are you going?" Misaki asked, grabbing Higotji's arm and pulling him back as he started a move toward the gorge.

"I have to help this creature."

"There are too many of them. Have you lost your mind? Or do you just want to die?" Misaki asked, in a frightened tone of voice.

"I can't stay here and watch this and do nothing about it."

"It's too dangerous, and we need to leave before we are surrounded, also," Misaki said, pleading with him.

"Stay here… and hide, if anything happens to me, just run and go back to the others. I'm going to help that creature," Higotji said. She let go of his arm, turned her head, and looked away. "Tell your mother that I'm grateful for her helping me. I'm also grateful to you, Misaki."

"I'm sure she didn't help you for you to go get yourself killed, like this." she replied as she was not happy with his choice.

"I'm only offering the same kindness that was shown to me," he replied. "If this is how I…"

"Don't say it," she said, stopping him. "Don't say it."

"Then, I guess this is goodbye, Misaki. Stay hidden, and don't let them find you," he said and stood.

Over to the ledge, Higotji lowered his body down and hung by his hands. His feet could not reach the bottom, so he reached over and grabbed a stone sticking out from the wall and eased himself further down, then dropped. He landed on his feet in the loose gravel of the gorge and took off running to help the creature. A sword in one hand and a rock in the other, he threw it into the crowd. The stone smacked one of the Cursed and bounced off hitting another. Several of them turned and saw him standing there. After him they went as he had interrupted their attack on the dragon. Faster and closer they came. Teeth snarling and claws out they ran with rage to engage him. He threw his sword and the point struck one in the face. Through the air his blade came rushing back into his hand. He gave it two quick swings slicing the second and third as the top of their heads fell off. Their bodies slid against the rubble and went motionless.

Higotji remained standing between the two dead bodies. The Cursed became enraged like a nest of hornets would after being disturbed. They growled as their attention turned toward him. He lifted his sword and threw another stone drawing many of them away from the creature. He readied his stance, closed his eyes, and took a slow breath to calm his mind and nerves. He could hear their feet scrape against the rubble as he gripped the blade's hilt. His brow tightened and eyes slowly opened again. He held the blade up covering part of his face. A claw swung at him, but he answered with a swing. His sword sliced it off and struck his attacker's head. Another came, he spun and stabbed it with the blade protruding from its face.

With the Cursed focusing to attack Higotji, the dragon shook its head, sending a few of The Cursed flying through the air. Now, with part of its head free, it was able to spit fire killing a portion of The Cursed. It then collapsed, being too weak to break the rest of its bindings to make an escape.

From behind and attacking quickly, one of the Cursed reached out for Higotji, but Misaki sliced its head in half before it could injure him. Turning quickly, he was surprised to see her, and asked, "What are you doing?"

"I'm saving your life again," Misaki said, stabbing another one that came up behind him. "I don't think my mother would approve of this."

"I won't speak a word of this to her," he replied as she stabbed one more in the head. He pivoted and swung his blade cutting another evil being down.

Misaki swung and twisted her blade. Her wrist flipped as she sliced and stabbed. Her strikes were perfect and precise. Every movement was fluid. She did not miss as she was trained by and had been married to a great swordsman. She spent hours with her mother and husband training for something like this. Together she and Higotji fought off the Cursed.

After slaying The Cursed, Higotji went cautiously over to the dragon as it whimpered and lay exhausted. Having never seen anything like it before, he reached out his hand to take off the dark material that bound the dragon. It had spread all over the dragon and kept it from moving. Though it was almost veil like, the material was as strong as hardened chain. At the end of the material, hooks held the claws of its wings to keep them from stretching out.

Misaki stood next to the dragon looking at its scales that were as colorful as a vibrant sunset. One of The Cursed came up behind to attack her, but seeing this, the dragon flicked its tail killing the evil monster. Misaki turned around to see the limp body which had a point sticking out from its face. Blood as dark as her hair ran down and dripped from the point. The dragon removed its tail and The Cursed fell to the ground without its face or brain.

Misaki took her sword and cut the material that was holding its feet bound. With a quick turn of its head, the creature made a squealing sound and snapped its jaws together causing Higotji to pull back his hand. Unsure if the dragon was going to try to kill him when it was freed, Higotji became hesitant to cut this creature loose. When he looked into the eye of the dragon, he saw his own reflection. Its eye focused on him as if he could see into the depths of the creature's spirit and hear its yearning. For a moment, he wanted to stand and stare back, but there was no time for it was struggling to breathe. Higotji took his blade and cut through the material loosening it from around its neck. The dragon took in a deep breath, exhaled slowly, and rested its head on the ground. Misaki removed the hooks, and the dragon extended it wings then brought them back in.

Barely alive, the dragon covered its legs as they turned a flesh color. Its wings made a cracking sound as the bones came together forming arms with hands and fingers. Its tail wrapped around its body and ruffled taking the shape of clothing. With a shake of its neck, the snout formed a face as it shape-shifted into a beautiful woman with long full wavy hair and the brightest blue eyes. The hair was red like her blood and reached to the middle of her back. Her scales finished turning into soft flesh that was pale and bleeding. Her clothing was a worn-out dress, white and wrinkled, now stained with blood and dirt. After the transformation, she was too weak to say anything. Wounded, exhausted, and losing blood, her eyes rolled back as she went limp, collapsed, and fell forward.

"I've got you," Higotji said. He dropped his sword and caught her to keep her from hitting the ground. He knelt with her in his arms and moved her hair away from her face.

"We need to leave immediately, before more of The Cursed start showing up or worse," Misaki said, with a concerned haste in her tone.

"Help me with her, she's bleeding," Higotji said

while he looked down at her and wiped blood from her mouth with his sleeve. The young woman had open gashes and teeth marks. She tried to keep her eyes open but was too exhausted. "What are we going to do?" asked Higotji.

"Let me think," Misaki replied looking around and sighing. "So, much for not saying anything to my mother."

The tip of her sword rested on the loose gravel. There was nothing obvious to be seen but rocks of various sizes in an open gorge. The wind blew gently and seemed to whisper softly. Misaki's hair rubbed slightly against her neck. It felt more like a gentle hand had moved it rather than the wind. She grabbed at her hair and neck turning rapidly to look over her shoulder, but nothing was there.

"Closer," the wind whispered but only to her. Misaki's eyes lifted and she saw the dark cavern at the upper edge of the gorge. She thought she caught a glimpse of a figure in the shadow move away to avoid being seen.

"Here, we can carry her," Misaki said, thinking quickly. She sheathed her sword and knelt. She put the young woman's arm around her neck. "Hurry now, put her arm around your neck and lift. We can carry her together."

"Let me grab my sword first," Higotji said. He

retrieved his sword, sheathed it, and placed his arm around the young woman's waist. They stood to their feet as they lifted her.

"Are you alright over there?" Misaki asked. The young woman's head hung over toward the ground.

"Yes," he replied.

"Alright, just keep her steady, I will do the same on this side," Misaki said, balancing herself.

"Good, let's get out of here and get her to your mother," Higotji said. They walked quickly toward the small ledge from which they had dropped earlier. The young woman's feet dragged against the ground as her body was still limp.

When they were many yards from the ledge, the wind blew again sending faint whispers. An eerie feeling came over Misaki. She could feel the creepiness of something in the shadows watching them. It made her angry and want to confront whatever was there. She looked over her shoulder as the wind blew again. Her eyes were drawn up to the cavern for one last glance. There she saw figures the same color as the forest. They dropped into the gorge and scratched the ground as they started running toward Misaki, Higotji, and the young woman. Dust from the gravel rose and stirred like a morning fog. She blinked then raised her dark eyebrows in terror. Her face lost its color as she gasped, and her heart raced. A great crowd of

The Cursed were running in a frenzy after them. She had never seen that many of them in her lifetime. As her mouth widened, she was unable to form words, let alone getting any to come out of the mouth. Her heart raced even faster as she picked up her pace to a jog. She almost left Higotji behind but they were held back by the young woman they were carrying. When Misaki looked back again, there seemed to be even more figures than before moving toward them. The Cursed were gaining on them. She faced back toward the ledge they had to climb to escape and screamed some words in her native tongue. Higotji looked over at her as his brow tightened, telling her, "I don't understand what you are saying."

"What do you mean you don't understand what I'm saying?" she replied. Pulling the young woman and moving quicker, she shouted again, "THE *Má Baé* ARE COMING! RUN!"

The End

of

Book Two

A

Sneak Preview

Into

Volume Three

Coming Soon!

CURSE OF
CROWNS®

THROUGH DEVILS EYE

GARRIS
L. R. COLEMAN

In This Life Or The Next, Never Trust a Bargolian!

CURSE OF
CROWNS

VOLUME THREE

THROUGH DEVILS EYE

Sneak Preview
of
Through Devils Eye

*U*nderneath the rolled, dried out skin of the map was a second layer. The Quartermaster bent the edge down and opened it up. The skins made a ripping sound as they were pulled away from each other. Once apart, they quickly rolled up by themselves and the first one flew out of his hand landing on the table. The second one, which was a light, yellow color, rolled and remained in his hand. He rolled out the skin and placed it on the table with small stones to hold the corners. It was another map with a complete paragraph on it in small cramped handwriting. His dark brown eyes moved side to side as he began to read the words. Suddenly, the table tilted as the ship rocked and the stones slid away from the map's corners. The Quartermaster braced against the table. A thud sounded from the impact at the front of the boat. A scraping sound was heard along each side of the ship. Stacks of scrolls fell from the table and rolled to one side of the room because of the hard impact. The wooden slats creaked and vibrated as the ship rocked. Underneath the floor, hard objects rolled knocking against the side of the boat. As the Quartermaster tried to keep things from going off the table, the ship calmed and returned to its normal course almost as quickly as the chaos came.

Peek straightened his back and looked for the stones that held the corners down, then he reopened the map with the writing again. He quickly flipped it upright and began to read. His forehead wrinkled as the inaudible whispers became clearer. He read aloud in his scratchy voice, "And near the Queen's tree is where the old ruthless King was betrayed. It was I, the one who was once his slave, who took the knife and plunged it deep into his back as he tried to take another form and leave. The ones that take our form enter through the Queen's tree, but I sit and wait for more of his kind to arrive, so that I can kill them also. Once the King was dead, I feasted on his blood and now my body will never age as his did. I have sat for years and have yet to see another shifter enter these lands. It was rumored that it was the old fool's blood that poisoned the tree and sealed it from any others entering, but I believe it also sealed the fate of the Queen for she would never have left her garden. Those that shape shift and take any other form should not be here where non-shifters live. They arrive claiming to create life, but soon turn vicious after being here for too long. If they are seen, do not hesitate to strike. They all must be killed."

Peek flipped over the map to see if anything else was written as his fingertips slid along the edges to see if it was stuck to another skin. He focused on studying the drawing of the Queen's tree. It showed a large trunk and appeared to have a tall mirror starting at the base, its limbs lifted to the sky. *I have seen that tree before, but its limbs hang down, not slope upward,* he thought to himself since it did not look like the tree he remembered. Many of the Bargolians tried to enter but were denied passage. It did not resemble any of the other trees for the pattern of its bark was diamond shaped scales that were black and gold. The leaves were tan colored and rattled when the wind blew. The slaves always knew when the King and Queen would arrive, for the leaves seemed to go into a state of confusion announcing their return. All the lands trembled with fear as the slaves never knew what was coming but only who was returning.

Peek's body lifted into the air. His knees came toward his chest as his feet went out. He dropped the map as everything seemed to rise and suspend in midair for a moment before coming crashing down. Peek landed onto his back and rolled. He tried to catch himself as he tumbled across the floor. He heard a loud crash behind him. He turned over onto his side to protect his body. The table broke free from the nails holding it to the floor. It slammed over onto its side and slid across the floor making a scrapping sound coming close to him. It turned at an angle and smacked against the wall cornering him. The ship rocked violently then came to a complete stop. Papers, scrolls, and a number of things that belonged to Mason scattered all over the cabin from the furniture coming loose.

Peek grabbed the edge of the desk grunting as he eased himself up to his feet. His breath was labored as he grunted again and put his hands on his back. A trickle of blood came down the side of his face. He wiped it and looked at his palm. The room was trashed, so he pushed the desk out of the way. He grabbed one of Mason's shirts and held it to his head for a while to stop the bleeding. *"What are they doing up there?"* he asked himself. Papers rustled as he looked for the two maps he dropped.

Moments later the latch turned, and the door swung open. Drift entered the room with haste quickly closing the door behind himself. Peek looked over at him as he was squatted down having just found the second map. Heavy running footsteps were heard above their heads on the main deck. Muffled shouts and metal clanking rang out as the ship was surrounded and was kept from exiting the port of Fog-shore. The sails continued to flap as they filled with wind but could not push them through the gates.

Below the main deck, Drift stood in the center of the room and extended his open hand. Between the desk and a turned over shelf, the Quartermaster looked back at him holding the rolled maps in his hand. Drift's forehead tightened as he squinted to see in the dim light of the cabin. He exhaled a deep breath and said, "I need those maps."

"Sir, what happened out there?" The Quartermaster asked.

"We are stuck between the gates of Fog-shore and can't get out. Everything we were planning has been compromised," Drift replied and extended his hand. "Now hand over those maps."

"Yes, Sir," he replied and stretched out his arm giving the maps to Drift. "Sir, your brother…"

"Yes, what of him?" Drift asked as he tucked the maps into his fur coat.

"Did he murder the King and Queen?"

Drift's raised his eyes, but his head remained down.

He kept his hand hidden inside the sleeve of the fur while adjusting the map. He looked back down toward his coat and replied, "And what if he did?"

"Are you saying Grahad killed the King and Queen?"

"The Queen knew that the King was dead when she took his powers. Thanks to the Queen we are all free from his grip. Grahad just finished his pathetic body off with a blade," he replied.

The Quartermaster stepped forward and stood facing him. Their eyes locked as his widened looking straight at Drift. He shook his head slightly as he sighed through his teeth and said, "Do you know what your brother has done? It wasn't the grip of the shape-shifting King and Queen you needed to be free from it was the shadow-shifters…"

"They all look the same to me, shadows, dragons, people, trees. They make no difference to me. If it shifts it needs to die," Drift replied.

"If the people back home find out what your brother has done, they may kill him themselves," the Quartermaster replied.

"They're not going to find out, because of that over there," he replied.

"What are you talking about?" the Quartermaster asked.

"Because of what's inside the box," Drift replied, his

eyes looked over to the side, behind the Quartermaster.

"What's inside the box?" he asked.

Drift looked back at him and raised his eyebrows but did not reply. The Quartermaster stared back at Drift then turned his head to look at the box in the corner of the room. His eyes went wide as he looked back forward. A gurgling sound came from his slightly opened mouth as the corners filled with a warm red. His body made a clunk as it went limp to the floor. Drift stood over him and pulled out the sharpened silver blade from his neck, shoved it in once again, followed by a few more times. Drift leaned over and said, "In this life or the next, never trust a Bargolian."

Drift withdrew the blade and flicked the blood from it then sheathed it inside his coat. He looked down at the lifeless body of the Quartermaster and nudged him over with his foot. Blood covered the floor as he lay motionless. He turned and walked toward the large closet as he said, "You learned too much, my friend."

He opened the closet door and slid the coats aside. There was a hidden latch to another door in the back. It creaked as he pushed it opened and climbed in. Drift slid the coats back into their place covering the secret passage as footsteps came closer. On the other side of the door, was another room where he sat and hid.

On the main deck feet scrubbed against the

flooring planks as the crew drew swords and readied themselves. With the ship trapped in the gates, the Fog-shore guards extended long wooden planks to board the ship. They kept their swords drawn and spears ready to strike down any who stood in the way. Other boats came and surrounded Mason's. Minutes went by as each side stared waiting for the other to make a move. On the dock, King Elias walked between guards with men he took from their families as Queen Sienna dealt with the others. At the edge of the docks, King Elias raised his hand and pointed. The men with him fell into the water. Many stood and watched as hands shaped like claws gripped the sides of the ship. Black and brown scales formed on their bare skin. Flickering tongues came out of their mouths as pointy heads moved from side to side. Their bodies slid along the wood. They all began to climb up the side of the ship.

Authors Note

Dear Readers,

Thank you to everyone who picked up a copy of Curse of Crowns volume two Blood You Will Taste and came back for a second journey. I hope you enjoyed it. I take this time and would like to invite you to leave an honest review or recommend it to a friend. Doing this always helps support your favorite Authors.

If you would like to stay up to date with new content and learn more about the worlds, characters, and artwork of Curse of Crowns, visit our website at www.curseofcrowns.com and sign up through email to receive all the latest content including book give away, book conventions, and of course new book release dates.

Thank you again for all your support.
Garris L. R. Coleman

ABOUT THE AUTHOR

Garris L. R. Coleman is the author of Curse of Crowns and enjoys writing fantasy fiction. Born in 1978, he grew up creating short stories ever since he could talk.

At the age of four, he picked up a pair of sticks and taught himself how to play drums and at age fourteen the guitar and began writing songs. When he is not writing or playing music, he enjoys spending time with his family and helping his wife homeschool their sons. He and his wife share their home in Georgia with their three entertaining sons.

Coming Soon!

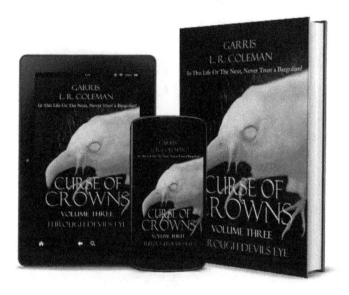

Book Three!!!
Through Devils Eye

Now Available!
Books 1 & 2

Also Available!
Curse of Crowns Merchandise!!!

www.curseofcrowns.com/store

CPSIA information can be obtained
at www.ICGtesting.com
Printed in the USA
BVHW080009010820
585163BV00001B/112